Hopeless Kingdom

Hopeless Kingdom

A.K. Koonce

To the Hopeless. May they bring us our salvation.

Table of Contents

Chapter One
Welcome to Juvar

The heavy shackles slam against my wrists the moment the anchor drops into the crashing waves. My hands fall in front of me with the weight of the chain and cuffs.

The warmth of the flames clinging to the crumbling buildings overwhelms my senses. Hot air surrounds me, and sweat begins to trickle down my spine.

Masses of people litter the muddy shore. Gray foam laps in from the dark sea, clinging to their legs as they wait for the occupants of this ship to descend. Big flakes of ash fall from the heavens, kissing my face as I hold my head high.

Pain shoots through my jaw from how tightly I'm clenching it together. The soldiers look at me with nervousness flashing in their darting gazes. They watch me closely even as they start to cuff Ryder, Daxdyn, and Darrio's wrists.

The three large and intimidating fae men hold their hands out submissively as they wait their turn for the shackles to bind their hands.

What the fuck is happening right now?

None of them meet my glaring gaze.

"What did you do?" I ask, my words clipping out through clenched teeth. My attention burns over Ryder and he still doesn't have the balls to look at me.

The soldiers look to Prince Ryder, waiting for his response.

He demanded I come here. This exiled prince insisted I bring them to the city of Juvar. Maybe he isn't in exile at all.

Daxdyn manipulates emotions. Apparently, he's much better at manipulation than I gave him credit for.

It's then that I look to Darrio. My throat tightens as I recall the way he opened up to me and I have to look away toward the billowing smoke of Juvar. The thick pollution chokes my airways even more with a mixture of uneven breaths and heavy betrayal.

I'm a fucking idiot.

But I'm not fucking helpless.

The light clinking of my chains is barely heard over the shouts from the residents on the coast.

"The Hopeless have returned to us. They have returned to save us all." It's a chant; an ominous and demanding chant that doesn't sound at all like admiration. It sounds like crying pleas. It sounds like screaming threats.

My hands clasp around the hilt of my father's sword, one finger after the other. I clutch it familiarly, comforted by the sense of belonging.

The pull of my arms lifting the sword sends my whole body into a fluid movement of defense. My arms tense into position. The blade held with aim, my core tightens and my legs crouch just slightly. Everything in me is fueled by survival.

These fae, who I almost trusted, just sold me out.

Friendship isn't comparable to revenge.

They think I was a shitty friend? Just wait until they see what a fucking atrocious enemy I can be.

The clanking of my chains signals my intent and the soldiers notice me a moment too late. My blade slashes through the ribs of one before the thundering of my boots carry me on to the next one. Three soldiers fall before I'm thrashing in Ryder's stunned face. Wide blue eyes look down on me.

"You did this. I trusted you, and you did this to me?" My voice is a shaking scream and the aim of my sword accompanies my words. The thick, iron chain binding his wrists comes up just in time to block the edge of my bloody blade.

With a quick jerking of his arms, he coils his chains around my sword until it tears from my palms and clatters to the damp wooden floor of the ship.

"Kara, stop," Daxdyn says, his warm arms rise above me and slip around me. The black chain on his wrists encompasses my body with my back pressing into his chest. His corded strength clings to my small frame. Anger shakes through my nerves.

I hope they burn here. I hope they all burn in the center circle of hell that is this destroyed city.

Ash settles on my tongue with every heaving breath I take and I force myself to just breathe; to just stop my thrashing and take a rational breath.

A bitter calm pushes into my chest, and the few

soldiers who are left stand with apparent tension in their posture. Everyone watches me with close attention.

When my eyes slowly open, I'm staring right at Darrio. The corners of his lips are turned down, and his steely gaze is filled with worry.

Regret is held there in his beautiful eyes.

Fuck him.

With a jarring movement, my head slams back into Daxdyn's perfect nose.

Pain soars through my skull but I don't pause to feel it.

A groan is heard with the sound of a satisfying crack of his nose.

I hope it heals with a slight angle.

He deserves more than just a small flaw on his absurdly gorgeous face but it's the best I can do at the moment.

He releases his hold on me, his hands coming up to cover the crimson blood that's gushing from his face. Then everyone on the ship is on me. My legs bend beneath their force. Their strong arms push me face down onto the damp floor. The smell of wood fills my senses as my cheek smashes into the deck.

"Zakara stop struggling. Just stop." Darrio's voice pushes past the angry shouts of the soldiers and it only fuels my aggression even more.

My teeth bite down sharply on an anonymous hand. My palm sneaks around the dagger strapped to my thigh and I manage to sink it into a shining black boot.

A stream of curses is all I hear just before one of them threads their fingers tightly through my long blonde hair. Pain shoots through my scalp and it's all I feel as he flings my head into the deck.

Ryder's quiet voice hums through my consciousness just as everything begins to blur.

"Trust me, Kara. Just trust me and everything will be okay," he says. The pleading sound of his voice sounds far off in the distance.

Then my heavy lids close to the blackness.

Chapter Two
A Prince and a Pawn

My eyes flutter open to more shadows, and I blink hard before I realize I'm actually awake. Throbbing pain stings through my skull, and I close my eyes once more. All around me is the beautiful sight of pure nothingness but I know where I am.

It's easy to identify a jail cell without really trying. The soft pads of my fingertips skim over the floor. My forearms pick up the grit of dirt, and my stomach sinks as I realize they've removed the cloth hiding the scars running up the inside of my wrist.

Metal grinds across the uneven brick floor. My hands are unshackled but strange cuffs remain around my wrists. The metal bites into my flesh, weighing my hands. Damp grime crumbles beneath my touch and my palms push down my jeans to wipe the dirty feeling away.

A consistent and shuddering sob echoes through the room. My heart pounds and I don't want to move. I don't want the others to know I'm awake. Taking a deep breath, moisture and mildew cloud my lungs. It forces me to clip my oxygen into small sips of air.

I stand and, without making a sound, I trail my hand along the iron bars. The cold feel of it skims across my fingers as my hand weaves in and out of each and every bar.

It's small; the size of one of Lady Ivory's walk-in closets.

The important thing is I'm alone. The others are locked away in different cells. I listen closely to try to count the number of cries I hear. Only one. If there are others, they aren't as weak as the loud man wailing into the night.

My muscles ache with intensity, but I make steady work of going over every inch of this space. Slowly, my fingers skim across each particle of dirt on the ground. When nothing is found, I begin to feel blindly at the smooth bars again.

A weapon.

That's what I'm searching for.

A loose screw or a sharp rock. If I'm ridiculously lucky a whole bar might wiggle free with a cruelly sharp point designated for Prince

Ryder's little lying heart.

I scoff at my dark thoughts and continue feeling up the bars one by one.

"There are no secret swords hidden away; not in your cell at least." A smooth, masculine voice that drips with self-satisfaction runs through the darkness.

The tension in my spine halts my movements as my eyes search the dense shadows.

"I was only admiring this beautiful room I've been given. Really know how to make a girl feel special," I say in a sensual voice. I push every ounce of sexual confidence I own into my words.

He isn't lying. They aren't handing out weapons to use. So, I'll have to use the only weapons I possess;

My alluring and delightful charisma, of course.

His laughter hums through the room, pushing over the fine hairs on my arm and shoving a disgusted shiver down my spine.

It's a laugh filled with mortal power.

The power to make someone fall to their knees and beg for their life.

"I'm glad you're enjoying your stay here, Miss Storm." More anxiety pushes into my chest at his simple use of my name. "I'd very much like you to enjoy all the true comforts I could offer you. Consider my home your home."

Repulsion fumes up my throat at the insinuation that's lacing his words. He isn't the first man to offer me *comforts within his home*, but he might be the last.

"You should answer the king when spoken to, Kara."

And there it is.

That voice that I once found to be the sexiest sound I'd ever heard. I hate the way my breath catches. I hate the way my thighs clench at the memory of him between them. I hate the way my heart feels like it's shattering into my lungs.

Darrio's here. With … the king. Are they all here? Are they all banding together to have one final laugh at the *fucking human* before she's sentenced to her soon-to-come death?

I thought they had a plan. Their destination was the Hopeless realm. Why did they go submissively into the heart of this city, right into the king's clutches?

Why?

The maddening question burns through me. I move toward where I heard their voices. My knuckles turn white as I clutch the bars, my face pressing between them to look up into the darkness.

"It'd be my pleasure," I say in a breathy voice. The tone says I'm gentle and vulnerable while my thoughts scream a song of pure hellfire vengeance.

I'll burn this fucking kingdom to the ground before I ever enjoy the *comforts* this prick could offer.

***

The white tile floor is stained with an abundance of dark, ashen footprints. The prints cross like a million soldiers have lost their way and stumbled blindly around this corridor. Dust clings to the extravagant silver light fixtures, dimming their shine. It's as if the smoke from this city is a burden on the lavish details of this enormous castle.

The building itself is familiar to me. This royal palace is held in my memories but I don't dwell on those memories.

That was a lifetime ago. So long ago I barely

remember any of it at all.

My hands hang at my sides and I make sure to keep them tucked close to my body, hiding the telling scars on my left arm the best I can. I keep an intentionally arrogant sway in my step. I'm free … but not. I feel my freedom locked away with every soldier that passes by. I note the sharp look they hold on my figure. I follow the stiff gait of Darrio, and the king of Juvar down the busy hall.

The king, King Tristan, is a needy little thing from the stories I've heard about him. I met him once before when he was only a prince. He was quiet and calculating even then. When his father passed away five years ago, he was young. A young ruler is bound to have flaws and Tristan didn't disappoint in that aspect. His pride and his ego are too large for the delicate golden crown that kisses his tidy dark hair. He made his self-importance abundantly clear when he retitled this city. Yes, he took the historical name that had graced this land for centuries and renamed it Juvar. Why? Because that was his dog's name and, apparently, he wanted his kingdom to know that even his lap puppy, Juvar, holds more importance than their miserable little lives.

I keep the disgust from touching my features and silently I follow behind the arrogant asshole.

The smooth white and gold wallpaper skims against the fingers of my right hand as I run them across the wall. Black soot flakes away, coating my skin. Three semi-white slashes trail behind me as I leave my mark down the halls.

Another soldier passes me, and a look of close scrutiny is all he gives me. A wicked smile curves my lips and I wink at him. His high cheeks flame red and his head tips low as he appraises my body with a heated gaze.

There's a pulsing knot on my temple from where the deck of the ship met my skull but from the look the man gives me, it must not be too horrendous.

If I could get close enough to one of them, I could steal the sword they keep within their weapons belt at their hip, or maybe the small knife there. Once I'm out of here, I'd have to sneak onto a barge, sail home and figure out how to remove these binding cuffs.

There's no lock in place on them, only perfectly smooth metal circling my wrists.

How odd.

The sound of the young soldier's boots drifts off down the hall and I don't realize we've stopped walking until Darrio's hard body meets my chest. Slowly his attention drifts down to me and his gaze shifts warmly across my features. The light gray color of his eyes isn't as hard-glaring as it was when we first met. They're filled with a look of concern.

He should be fucking concerned.

My arms fold across my chest and I step back from him, my jaw set so tightly it hurts. I hold his stare until he's forced to look away.

We stand before a wide, glossy door. King Tristan's pale hand grips the gold handle and pushes it open. Walking inside, he holds it open for Darrio and me.

Pure calculation is all that thrums through my body. My eyes skim over every detail of the room; the tarnished locks that are in place on the high arching windows, the stain of dark smoke hides the outside world from my view. Books of every shape and size line the walls. A black carpet sits askew at the center of the room. A long, glossy table fills the area with two dozen chairs lining the sides. Several men and women talk quietly but I don't linger on their faces and murmuring voices.

Because there, in the far corner, hidden among the shadows, is a suit of display armor. A knight's armor stands proudly. It's simply décor to these people. But to me, it's what I've been searching for.

A weapon.

Held loosely and carelessly between the decorative knight's metallic hands is a long, majestic sword.

It could be nothing; a minor detail among the grand scheme of things. Or it could be the very thing that takes King Tristan's life.

"How nice of you to finally join us, Zakara." A woman's delicate voice pulls at my attention. My gaze shifts slowly from the promising sword and lands on the one who spoke my name.

Full red lips smile coyly at me while deep brown eyes gleam with hidden cruelty. The length of her chestnut hair is curled softly at the ends as if she's an angelic dream woman who can't possibly be real. A thinly wired crown gleams at her temple. The diamond at the center of it shines with pride even in the minimal light of the room.

My thoughts assess everything about her.

She's beautiful.

She's regal.

She's the queen.

"My Queen," Tristan says in a hushed tone as he places a quick kiss against her cheek. She leans into that small fraction of affection. She practically glows from it.

Tristan takes a seat at the head of the table, his attention falling to me once more. A seriousness moves across his features. A soft ticking sound trails through the room and my gaze follows a small dog with coarse gray hair. Tiny legs carry its wide little body over to the king, and he sweeps the animal up into his arms.

It's the first time I've really looked at the king in the hazy light.

It's hard to believe Ryder and Tristan share blood. Nothing about them is remotely similar and yet, they have the same father.

Inky black locks are pushed back from his face. A carefully groomed amount of facial hair lines his upper lip and chin and curves the sharp edges of his jaw. Wicked power shines in his emerald eyes.

"I would have joined you sooner, but I was a little ... detained." Confidence stiffens my spine.

Laughter rumbles through the room. It's a light and familiar sound that tingles across my skin.

My attention falls to the sound of his humming amusement.

Daxdyn Riles looks to me with a smile that melts me.

I hate how his uninvited happiness sinks right into me.

Fucking empath powers.

A light bruise shadows the bridge of his nose. It isn't awful looking. It certainly doesn't take away from his strong and attractive features.

Why do I suddenly feel guilty for hurting him? I shove the churning feeling aside.

The gray in Daxdyn's eyes looks different. His happiness still shines within them, but sadness emits from just beneath the surface. That look sinks into me, and he shifts in his wooden chair until he's staring down at his hands that he holds atop the glossy table. He's seated at the end, the farthest away from the king and queen, but closest to me.

Darrio stands to my right, not leaving my side. The warmth of him seems to radiate into me, making me abundantly aware of his strong presence.

My gaze trails the wide room until I spot the

last one.

Prince Ryder leans against a towering bookshelf. The warm sunlight that manages to peek through the grimy windows shines in his narrowed sea blue eyes. The bulge of his muscles catches my attention as he stiffly folds his arms across his wide chest. The blonde locks of his hair are disorderly and pushed back from his gorgeous face.

Anger rolls off of him in violent slashing waves.

"Pay no attention to my pouting big brother." King Tristan's amused voice travels up the vaulted ceiling and lingers.

Big brother. The term 'step mother' circles my memory.

Are they step siblings?

Thoughts fly through my mind as my gaze stays on the smooth features of my prince.

My prince?

Hardly. I swallow dryly, confused by the affectionate term.

It is interesting that Ryder's father was the ruler of this land, and yet his younger step brother now owns the crown.

This fae was pushed out of his kingdom. Exiled into the Hopeless realm at a very young age. *Did he come back for his father's funeral five years ago?*

"Ryder, you cannot let a woman ruin our budding friendship." The king pins him with a sneering look.

Are they talking about me?

The ridges of Ryder's back tighten, bunching together with tension that's beginning to fill me as well.

"Queen Anna didn't ruin our relationship, Tristan." His black boots swivel against the tile until he's staring hard at the queen. "The lies she used to lure the three of us from the Hopeless realm were your own." His gaze hardens and his twisting smile sinks a peculiar feeling into the pit of my stomach. "Did your wife relay everything back to you?"

"Of course, she did. Everything she did was my own doing, Ryder. Your relationship was a pawn placed by my own hand."

That haunting smile turns crueler. "Did your pawn tell you how often she choked on my dick, or was that just improvised? When she met me in the forests at midnight here, begging for me to fuck her, was that a perk for the pawn?" The flashing anger is mixed with amusement in his eyes.

My brows rise at his bold words. Ryder ... slept with Tristan's wife. In an instant, my gaze swings to the high and mighty king and his whorish queen. Shame reddens Anna's ivory skin. The tops of her breasts push against the silk corset that's restraining her heaving breaths.

"Do not speak of my queen in that tone. Our father would be ashamed of you, brother." The cooled expression he gives Ryder is one of complete control.

"I'd think it was the colorful description he gave rather than the tone that it was given in," I whisper on a bubbling laugh. My jaw snaps shut with realization.

Oh, my gods, why did I say that?

A coughing laugh falls from Daxdyn's lips just as Darrio turns to give me a stunned look that says 'are you fucking serious right now'. Ryder smiles at me, and the feel of his happiness flutters through my nervous stomach.

The attention in the room falls back on me; the idiot prisoner with the big mouth.

"Have they been good to you, the fae?" Tristan asks. He looks at me with intense interest. In fact, no one's ever looked at me the way King Tristan does. Sexual lust isn't in him. It might not exist in this sleazy man at all. He looks at me the way he probably looked at that crown that once sat atop his father's head. He looks at me as if I'm a thing of power.

And now he owns me.

The sound of my boots shifting fills the deliberate silence. I let my lashes flutter down to admire the harsh cuffs that adorn my wrists; bracelets of imprisonment. Suddenly I notice all four of us are wearing matching cuffs as if at any minute they might shackle us once again.

The time I spent with the three fae skims through my thoughts like a soft caress against a painful scar.

"They were very charming. Thanks for asking." I flash a short-lived smile before pulling my lips tightly closed.

Tristan stands, ignoring everyone including his tainted wife. The sound of his heavy steps striding toward me sinks dread through my body with every echoing move he takes.

The twisting feeling within my stomach is swallowed down as I steel my spine and wait for whatever displaying act he's about to perform.

Thin fingers push back a lock of my blonde hair, and it's then that I realize lust is very much alive within this man. It might be a mangled, dominant, abused form of sexual frustration, but it is in fact a living, breathing, disgusting thing within him.

"I want you to join me for dinner tonight." His fingers trail down my jaw and a crawling shiver scurries down my spine. "I have something I want to show you." My teeth smash together as I let him stroke my skin.

Despite my nerves, my stomach growls at the mention of dinner. My gaze trails back to the hazy window. Clouded hues of deep orange threaten to shine through. How long was I out for? It's nearly sunset now. Was it only a few hours or a few days?

Darrio shifts forward, his shoulder bumping in to Tristan's. The king's hand falls back to his side and I release a tense breath.

"Darrio, I'd like you to keep an eye on our little … guest. You're turning out to be a man of loyalty." He turns from me, giving Darrio's impressive size a once over. "Prove your loyalty to me." He clasps his hand on the fae's bulky shoulder as he stares up at him.

I peek at Darrio, wondering if he's scowling as always.

A genuine smile is all he possesses. Darrio's teeth are white and straight and flash with humor that I've never seen before. It makes him handsome. His smile dissolves the scars lining his face, and the dark beard shadowing his jaw only smooths his rough edges into something of pure carnal sexuality.

I'd be attracted to him even more if I wasn't still nauseated by his betrayal and from King Tristan's closeness.

"I'd be honored, my King." The obedience in Darrio's deep voice washes away every speck of attraction I previously held for him.

Fucking traitorous fae.

I keep my eyes on the floor as King Tristan's hungry attention drifts over me. I feel it clawing into me, turning my stomach with the feel of his gaze.

Off the top of my head, I can think of a hundred different times I've used my appearance to my benefit. But, I also know when I'm toying with a stupid boy and when I'm tiptoeing around a very, very dangerous man. King Tristan is the latter of the two.

He's filled with more danger than he is desire.

But so am I.

Chapter Three
Help

Once again, I mark the halls of this castle with two fingers this time. I trail a path from what appeared to be the dining hall to the room that Darrio's leading me to.

"Making a path?" Darrio asks, his pace slowing to fall in place at my side.

I continue to let the soot stain my hand as I brush the dirty wall with my fingertips. His gaze burns across my skin, but I refuse to give him the satisfaction of my attention or a response.

"You don't have to leave a trail. We won't be sticking around, Kara."

This information has me perking up and I chance a glance at him.

His silver gaze holds mine and his lips part like he might say more, but he doesn't. He isn't Daxdyn; he won't spill his guts to me without being prompted.

"If you are a trusted and loyal servant now," I pause letting a smirk kiss my lips as I taunt him, "why are you wearing the cuffs?"

We stop outside a door that might be mahogany, but it's covered in so much charcoal colored dust that it's hard to tell.

"They're iron. Iron stunts fae magic. It's harboring my powers. The king wants us to return to our places. He wants fae at his disposal as they once were all those decades ago. It's best if we let him believe that's what's happening."

He takes one hand and rubs it over the smooth iron clasping his other wrist.

"Guess a fire fae can only be trusted so much," I muse as my fingers drop from the wall.

This is my room. I can tell by the way he keeps glancing toward it. A long torturous sounding breath leaves his lips as if there are words pressing against his chest, pushing to get out.

"I guess I'll see you tonight when you pick me up to deliver me to your king." The intentional twist of my words fuels my anger. "Will you carry me right to his bed?" His jaw tics, struggling to remain closed, so I push a little harder. "Will he make you undress me for him?"

"Kara, stop," he grinds out through clenched teeth.

A single step is all I take toward him, letting my chest brush against his as he glares down into my fuming gaze.

"Maybe he'll even let you watch," I whisper in a shaking breath that barely maintains my emotions.

Then he's shoving me. My back hits the wall and his body covers every inch of mine. He holds himself on his arms above my head as he stares down at me, his warm breath fanning between us. The feel of his thrashing heart shakes into me, and it dictates my own heartbeats until they mirror one another, beat for beat.

He tilts his head low, his lips just a breath away from mine.

"Don't ever think that I would allow his fucking hands to touch you." His promise is spoken in a rage-filled whisper. Fury shines in his eyes like I've only ever seen when he used his powers on the soldier who lost his face to Darrio's magic. Would the simple cuffs on his wrists really prevent that raw power from leaving him?

His attention falls to my lips, and for a second,

I remember he hasn't kissed me since I slapped him. Desire spreads through me with that thought alone. He and I have this tension between us like I've never felt with anyone else. The way his body's aligned with mine, the energy I feel pooling through him, it has me shifting my thighs against his.

The thoughts are smothered out as I realize he's the reason I'm here at all. I'm a prisoner of the Kingdom of Juvar because he lied to me.

"If you don't intend to tell your king that, then I suggest you stop looking at me as if I'm yours, *Rio*."

Harshly, I shove against his chest, pushing past him. The door eases open under my touch, and I don't look back at him as it closes behind me. My head leans back against the door and a shaking sigh parts my lips. Wet tears sting my eyes, but I breathe out the emotions until the tightness in my chest dissolves into a manageable feeling.

The noise that clicks through the room is so quiet I barely hear it. But I do hear it; the sound of a lock clicking in place.

Just like a good little servant, Darrio Riles just locked me in my room.

The frustration in me simmers as I take in my new lavish jail cell.

The room is elegant. Fresh, white blankets line the enormous bed. It looks soft and inviting, the nicest bed I've ever seen, actually. A small sitting area takes up most of the space. Two swooping loveseats face each other. A worn wardrobe stands at the far end of the room, and in the opposite corner is a shining claw foot tub. Everything is open. There's not a single place to hide in the room. And, upon closer inspection, not a single extra weapon is gifted to me. I'm allowed one towel, several choices of outfits and, for whatever reason, a basket of cookies.

They really rolled out the welcome wagon here. A heavy sigh parts my lips as I scan over my room once more.

The balcony window chants my name on repeat and my feet carry me to it the moment I hear Darrio's boots fade away down the hall.

There's no lock!

There's no fucking lock on the balcony doors.

Oh, could they be so stupid?

The glass doors swing open with an announcing shriek of the hinges, and my fingers grip the cold stone railing. Down, down, down my gaze travels. Darkness eludes the depths of the earth. I'm so high up I cannot see the ground. The tips of flames can be seen in the distance; smoke and darkness is all that greets me.

This land was once my home. I squint against the smoky clouds. The small cottage I grew up in with my father flashes through my mind and I try to imagine it as one of the rooftops outlined in the distance.

Wishful reminiscing is all it is. And I don't have time for fond memories at the moment.

I step closer to the edge and find that the surface of the building is rough concrete, but entirely flat. Not one handhold is offered to me. I peek up at the space above me to find one more floor. A balcony is just above, and several high yards above it is the slate black roof.

Okay … if I can't go down … I should go up?

Up is better than having to go down … on Tristan.

That thought sours my stomach, but it gets my feet moving quickly enough. I hoist myself up on the smooth rail and balance my weight. My stomach twirls uneasily, and I hug my thin frame to the wall. I'm not afraid of heights but the mysterious darkness below makes plenty room for fear to trickle in. Concrete scuffs my cheek as my long hair dances recklessly in the wind.

On the toes of my boots, I reach for the balcony above. I teeter, stretching to the fullest of my meek height. The cool breeze is all that meets my fingertips. It's about five feet from my reach. A shaking breath skims through my clenched teeth, and the image of Tristan's cruel mouth fuels my movements. On a last-ditch effort, I leap for it.

The smoky air catches my body in the gentle winds, shooting heart-pounding fear all through me.

But it isn't enough.

I land hard on my knees. My palms sting into the floor of my balcony. Slowly, my eyes close as I stay hunched on the ground.

I breathe deeply through my nose.

It's alright. It's fine. I just won't be using this room as an escape route.

A mantra of calming thoughts circles my mind as I stand and dust off my torn jeans. I don't bother closing the door behind me. I want to fume on it a bit longer.

Storming across the room, I turn on the faucet to the tub. The white porcelain is too cold for comfort, and I turn the hot water on to its fullest. I undress as I pace. A trail of my clothes litters the room, and I continue to glare daggers at the balcony even as I slip into the deep bathtub.

The cold structure of the bath fights against the steaming hot water spilling into it. I sink low, letting my head disappear beneath the clear water. With my eyes tightly closed, my muscles relax and I let my thoughts drift.

Why would they do this? Why would they bring me here? Is the Hopeless realm really why we're here?

They seem free while I'm living as a luxurious prisoner of Juvar.

A whore.

That's what I'll be.

I push harshly against the bottom of the slick tub until air meets my lungs. Water trails down my shoulders and chest as I push my hair from my face.

As soon as my eyes open, they land on his smile.

Daxdyn's heated gaze follows a line of water that's falling down between my breasts. My thighs clench together, and I force myself not to shy away from the look in his eyes. My fingers clench into my palms at my sides.

He sits on the edge of the tub, near my feet. Dark locks fall into his lashes as he stares at me with hooded eyes.

A thousand snarky thoughts drift through my mind, but only one seems to fit here in this moment.

"Pass the soap," I say in a steady but breathy voice.

White teeth sink into his lower lip as his gaze trails down my body to the column of my throat, my smooth round breasts, my scarred ribs, heating across my navel. His attention stops as I bring my legs up slightly in the warm waters to hide what I know he's looking for.

Surprisingly he doesn't drop the soap like I thought he might. He hands the little white bar over, our fingers tingling with contact. A muted feeling of his emotions flows through me, driving right down to the center of my sex.

I shiver, but remain focused on the task of

pushing the soap across my dirty skin. When it's nearly overflowing, he turns the faucet off for me.

With rapt attention, he watches in silence. It's strangely erotic. A tightness pebbles my nipples as I push the lathery soap across my chest and down my stomach. A heavy sigh drifts over my lips like a quiet moan, and my breath catches more when I see his hand fall to the crotch of his straining jeans. He adjusts himself stiffly.

Up and down his chest rises and falls. I pause, my legs angled closed, the bar held just below my hip bones. An energy burns between us as we stare hungrily at one another. In this moment, he's at his weakest.

It's then that I strike.

"Why did you bring me here, Daxdyn?" His name is a rasping breath on my tongue.

A smirk tilts his lips, and he clears his throat before looking away from me.

"Let me help you and I'll consider telling you."

Help. Never in my life has that word sounded less like a kindness and more like a kinky foreplay.

A pooling wetness that has nothing to do with the water heats between my legs.

"Fine."

His brows raise high like it's the last thing he ever expected me to say.

Without further warning, he begins pulling at the back of his white shirt. His slim waist leads up to panes of hard muscle. Inch by inch his body of lithe strength is revealed to me. He shakes out his hair and holds my gaze as he begins unfastening his belt. The light clinking of metal fills the silence before he lowers his black jeans to the ground. A thick hardness shadows beneath his dark briefs, and I shift involuntarily within the waters.

The strain he puts on the thin material of his boxers has me rising up a little as his thumbs hook into the elastic band around the veering lines of his hips.

"No." The traitorous word blurts from my mouth.

"No?" he repeats slowly, still gripping the top of his boxers.

"Those stay on. You're helping *me*, remember?"

A humming groan rumbles through his chest as he breathes out a smile.

"Right." He nods his head as he begins to stalk toward me. "I'm here to help you." His words are spoken pointedly. He lowers himself into the tub, his arms caging me in as he holds himself above me, gripping the sides of the bath. My legs fall open with a rush as he lowers himself between my thighs. "I'll help you forget how angry you are."

The corded muscles of his arms are cut with lines as he holds his weight above me. He's all around me but barely touching me.

"I doubt that," I say with a smile.

His lips brush over my damp hair as his hips finally settle against mine. The hardness tucked away within his drenched boxers drags against my sensitive folds. "I'll help you so good, you'll forgive me," he whispers.

Another gentle rock of his hard dick against my clit has my eyes fluttering closed, my heartbeat pounding loudly.

The warmth of our bodies fades away as he pulls back from me. With hazy eyes, I stare up at him as he kneels between my legs. He licks his lips slowly and his gaze trails down my bare skin. Every inch of me is exposed like an offering to him. A teasing skim of his index finger against my inner thigh has me shaking beneath his minimal touch.

The soap pulls from my palm as he glides it down my body. He takes his time, letting his fingers explore the soft skin of my inner thigh and down the long length of my leg. My heart pounds at the feel of his skimming touch. I smile as he lathers up my feet before cupping water to rain down on my skin, washing away the glistening bubbles.

The water's barely warm now. My hair hangs in pale, cold strands against my shoulders.

The heated look in his eyes meets mine as he lifts my left leg and places it against his shoulder. My slick skin meets his and my lips part with an unsteady breath. A gentle kiss feathers across my calf as his strong hands hold my thigh. Hot breath fans across my skin as the soap sinks to the bottom of the tub, forgotten.

Ever so slowly, his palm lightly trails up the length of my leg; over my knee, along my inner thigh and he circles the soft skin there before he finally brushes over my most sensitive spot.

His attention sinks into me, soaking up every one of my emotions.

I physically feel his gaze heating my face as he

watches me with flaring attention. My eyes fall closed as his fingers push up and then down, tightening that feeling deep inside me. A shaking gasp leaves my lips as he sinks two fingers into me. His palm rubs over my clit with every leisurely stroke of his fingers.

Everything in my life slips away as he makes me forget with the steady pace of his demanding hand.

He was right; I do forget how angry I was.

My legs shake as he begins to pound harder into me. The waters of the bath begin to lap against my chest with the rhythm of his movements.

"Come for me, Kara," he demands, stroking me faster, rubbing perfect pressure against my clit. Roughly, his other hand grips my hip, holding me in place for him.

A moan pulls from me at the tone of his voice, the sound of it drifts through the room. The hard edge of the tub meets the back of my head as my spine bows against the waters. A shaking cry is all I have when he arches his fingers and my sex clenches tightly, my legs shaking in the cold water.

Waves of pleasure course through me, and I soak up the feeling while Daxdyn watches every second of it.

The feel of his fingers slipping from me is grounding. My eyes flutter open just as he leans forward and presses a kiss to my inner thigh. His hot tongue skims across his lips, flicking against my skin. Another incoherent sound slips from my mouth. A look of fire burns in his hooded eyes as he places another hot, teasing kiss to the soft skin of my inner thigh.

I feel weak. Weak and powerful all at once.

"Daxdyn." His eyes flare at the sound of his rasping name on my lips.

His hand drifts through the soapy water and rests low on my hip, his body angling closer to mine; poised for whatever it is I might say next.

The rise and fall of his chest is his only reply as he waits eagerly for me to finish my sentence. I'm spread out before him, my calf still resting against his shoulder.

"Tell me why you brought me here."

Slowly his eyes close as a smile spreads over his features.

"You are persistent, do you know that?"

Daxdyn makes it hard not to like him, not to

trust him entirely. But I try anyway. I untangle my body from his and step from the tub, water trails across the hardwood floors as I let the cool air dry my skin. The feel of his gaze on my body makes my hips sway a bit more than usual as I walk to the wardrobe.

The doors open without a sound. About a dozen dresses hang neatly within.

No jeans.

I enjoy a pretty dress as much as the next thief, but they aren't very tactical.

A short black dress with silky material greets my fingertips, and I rip it from the hanger without further thought.

Daxdyn settles in against the back of the tub, occupying my previous spot. Water glistens against the crevices of his chest. A boyish, but cocksure smile fills his face.

Gods above, he's too sexy for his own good.

An hour ago, I wanted to murder him. One soapy orgasm later and he made good on his promise; I do forgive him.

For the moment.

The dress slips over my head, hiding my body

from his hungry gaze.

I adjust my hair, raking my fingers through the damp locks.

He eyes my long legs as I take a seat on the end of the bed, crossing one ankle over the other. I am the epitome of a classy lady.

"No panties?" Daxdyn pipes up from his spot in the bathtub.

Classy. Lady.

I pick carelessly at my nails.

"It appears that they think a pair of underwear might be used as a weapon. Or, the king is just a fucking pervert."

He nods his head, his arms encompassing the edge of the tub as he leans back and gets comfortable.

"Probably both," he tells me with a serious look.

Worn leather meets my fingertips and I tug on my boots as if I'm getting ready to leave this wicked prison at any moment.

"You helped me, now tell me."

"Seems like a win-win for you." Daxdyn's confidence seems to heighten when he's nearly naked. I thought he was arrogant before, he's nothing but lazy assurance right now.

"I believe you're the one who asked to help. It certainly didn't look like you got nothing out of the deal."

He gives another sultry smile that makes me smirk at him. Things are simple between us. He just has a personality that draws people to him.

I'm drawn to him.

Finally, he looks away, toward the open balcony door. Is Daxdyn my neighbor in the room above this one?

"A little over a year ago, Ryder met this human here in Juvar. They were screwing around a lot, but Darrio told him she'd get him in trouble. He agreed it'd be best to end things. Darrio and I went with Ryder, safety in numbers and all that," he pauses when I give him a skeptical look. "Human women are a bit … kinder than fae women." Another long pause as my eyes narrow on him.

It's hard for me to imagine all three of them needing to come here. Unless …

"You all came here, risking your lives, to get

42

laid? Are you saying human women are easy?"

Laughter rumbles through his chest as he tilts his head up toward the ivory ceiling.

"Not the word I'd use, but," he shrugs a little. "Anyway, he was going to break up with her. The three of us met in the forest that borders our realm and this one, but she wasn't there. Anna wasn't there. Ryder's step mother was, though. The former queen was waiting."

His look becomes serious as he studies the dirty lines of the hardwood floors.

"Poison darts were the last thing I remember. We woke up in the tower you found us in."

"What did she want?"

His gaze fills with sadness when he finally looks up at me. A line creases his handsome face. In the quietest of voices, he says something that makes my heart skip a beat. It fills my veins with a fear unlike anything I've ever experienced before.

"You."

Chapter Four

The Traveler

Confusion and fear swirl through me like violent winds. My lips part to ask him the millions of questions circling my head just as the door swings open.

Darrio stands, filling the frame entirely. The silver of his gaze drags from me, sitting leisurely on my bed to his brother who, of course, is still relaxing nearly naked in the bathtub.

The two share a strange look between themselves, a silent communication that I'm not included in.

"King Tristan wants your presence now." Darrio's attention falls hard on me, but there's no judgement in his gaze. It doesn't stop my arms from folding across my chest to keep them steady. Not a single question about the odd scene before him is asked.

He's a man of few words and fewer cares, I suppose.

Will Darrio really just lead me to his king as if I mean nothing to him?

"Come, Kara."

Come for me, Kara.

I push the rasping dirty echo of Daxdyn's voice away with a shiver shaking my shoulders.

A squeaking sound accompanies my steps and I realize Daxdyn and I might have lost some water during playtime.

"I'll see you soon, Kara," Daxdyn says in a light tone. He makes it sound like everything will be okay. His voice almost makes me believe that.

I turn the hall with Darrio. Before we leave, he twists a golden key into the lock and locks his brother within my rooms. My brows raise but I don't question it.

Hell, at least I'll have someone who I almost trust waiting for me when I return.

If I return.

He leads the way in silence and when we begin a new route through the dark halls of the castle, I make sure to trail a line with my index finger down the corridor.

Three leads to my cell.

Two leads to the dining hall.

And one … one line leads to what I'm anticipating to be a very violent show.

"Stop marking your spot. I already told you, we won't be here long," Darrio says in a hushed voice. His steps are pure confidence; a swagger that says 'people don't fuck with me'.

He's enormous and has absolutely nothing to fear.

While I'm all of five foot five with the muscle tone of a small, but very aggressive bunny.

My jaw clenches shut and, before I can think better of it, I push him. To my surprise, he stumbles under my small touch. Adrenaline rips through me and I shove him again until he's against the wall.

A nagging voice in my mind says he lets me, but I ignore the little voice of reason.

On my tippy toes, I lean into him until I'm right in his face. The dark, trimmed strands of his beard glisten under the dim lighting and the shine of his depthless eyes holds a look of concern masked with boredom.

"Maybe we won't be here long, but at the moment, you're about to feed me to the wolves without any protection whatsoever." A shaking sound fills my voice and I breathe hard to make that weakness disappear from within me.

Large hands settle on my hips, calming me with the simple connection of his body and mine. I want to hate him. I want to hate them all so badly, but that fuming anger just isn't there when he's looking at me like it hurts his heart to hurt me.

"I'd never let anything happen to you." The quiet rumbling promise of his voice melts my ovaries; I swear it. I don't know how Darrio and I got here. I can't say when our relationship took this turn. But when he promises to protect me, I believe him. "What you said earlier about claiming you as mine." His gaze dips to my lips and my hands settle over his broad chest. His heart pounds wildly against my fingertips. "You're not mine, but you are *my fucking human*."

A small smile tugs at the corner of my lips, and it reflects in his eyes until fine lines crease the corners there with nothing but real happiness showing in his face.

I like the idea of being his fucking human. I've been his fucking human since we first met but now it's a term of affection … I think.

The emotions in me grow until I have to shove them back down into the darkness of my heart.

Emotions are dangerous, and I can't afford to feel them right now.

"If you lead me into danger," I stroke my fingers across the swooping ink lining his collar bone as I speak in a sweet whisper, "your fucking human will kill you." It sounds like a loving promise. In a way, it is; a loving, but sincere, promise.

A rumbling laugh shakes through his chest and his hand falls to my lower back. For only a second my hips are pushed into his, sending a twirling energy through my core.

"I'd expect nothing less."

The warmth of his big hand sears against the small of my back as he pulls away and leads me down the quiet hall. My hip brushes his, our sides touching coyly. And ever so gently, with nimble fingers, I pull the small black knife from his belt.

It's military standard; just like my father used to have. The royal emblem is engraved into the hilt of it, my fingers brushing against it for only a second.

One seemingly careless stumble later and I've

hidden it away within my right boot.

I flash the man I care far too much about an embarrassed smile as he helps me to my feet.

Anger still pounds through my heart. It beats in time with the sound of our footsteps as he leads me closer and closer to what will most definitely be an entertaining dinner.

***

Dinner is … rather boring, actually. My spine stays glued to the back of my seat; tension fills my shoulders as I wait for the veil to be pulled away from this eerily mundane situation.

This room is the largest I've seen so far. To my left, Tristan sits at the head of the table. His food goes untouched as he stares hard at me. I feel his attention boring into the side of my face as I pretend to feign interest in my salad. The delicate green leaves haven't touched my lips but I push them around nonetheless. It's a shame to let possibly poisoned food go to waste, really. The wine at the corner of my plate tempts me, but I don't take one sip. I'll drink the dirty bath water Daxdyn's keeping warm for me before I chance a drink of that.

An older woman with streaks of silver cast

down her long ebony hair stares wide eyed at me as well. She's the former queen. I haven't seen her since my father died protecting me from her when my Hopeless scars first appeared. Her gaze makes me shift slightly in my seat, but still I don't look at her.

Across from me, Ryder sits in silence, his hands clasped over his plate. Dark metal peeks out on his wrists from beneath his snug, long sleeve shirt. A spasm in his tightly held jaw tells me he's counting down the seconds until we are dismissed.

"She's quieter than I thought she would be," the king muses. His comment still doesn't pull my attention to him but I notice Darrio nodding carelessly along with Tristan's words. "No man ever complained of a silent woman. Am I right, Darrio?" Self-assured laughter accompanies the king's words.

Not one second passes and a chuckling sound rumbles through Darrio as he nods even more, taking a large drink of wine. "Right you are, your Highness."

I study each individual prong of my silver fork. The shine of it catches my attention as I fist it in my palm, resisting the urge to embed the utensil deep in Darrio's muscular thigh.

Asshole.

"I like you, Darrio. You're not at all like your brother," Tristan says and once more Darrio nods in agreement. The more he speaks to Darrio, the more I want to climb my ass on top of this table and slit the king's throat with a butter knife. "The other one, the aggressive fae with the lashing attitude, he'll be allowed out of his rooms once he learns not to threaten my life again."

Daxdyn threatened his life? He didn't mention that. He could have spared a moment during—after my orgasm to note that important detail.

I arch a brow at the thought. *The aggressive one.* Doesn't really seem like Daxdyn. He has it in him, but what could have set him off to make him a prisoner just like me?

To my right, Darrio shoves heaping spoonfuls of mashed potatoes into his mouth like he's trying to close the hole in his face with impossibly large portions of food. I cock a brow at him but, apparently, my judgment doesn't affect his dinner. Another overflowing bite is shoveled right in.

Gods above, where is he putting it?

"Do you know why you're here, Zakara?" Tristan's voice halts Darrio's obnoxious eating. His spoon lowers stiffly to the edge of his plate.

Thank the fucking gods.

My gaze swings over the few people seated, and I make note that Queen Anna is not present. Then my attention falls on the man with the burning interest sparkling in his eyes.

"I just assumed it was a vacation of sorts. You have a very interesting way of making a woman feel welcomed here." A tight smile is forced to my lips.

"You are very welcomed here. I apologize for the unfortunate first impression I made, but I had to be sure of who you were." His attention drifts down my body, sending a crawling feeling over my skin. "I have someone I want you to meet."

"Traveler, please join us," the king's mother whispers in a breathy voice. A voice filled with passion that makes her eyes flutter closed. Her thin fingers sweep across a shining pendant that's hanging from her neck. She worries at the necklace as if she's putting all her faith into the trinket.

I can't explain it but the moment she says it, I feel the veil finally slip away. A chill settles into the large dining room. The feeling claws under my flesh and sets my nerves into a frenzy.

Soft steps echo through the silence and my attention searches the dimly lit room. Darrio's hand lowers with discreet slowness to his hip. His fingers fumble over the empty sheath and his gray eyes narrow on me when he realizes his weapon is missing.

Ryder keeps his head down, but I can physically feel his faded energy. His magic wants to shudder him in and out of this setting. Would he leave us?

Leave me?

"If your pet is smart, he'll keep his distance," Ryder says, not looking toward his step brother.

Pet.

The word lingers between us and I stare at him in confusion until I see it.

He isn't a man. At least, I don't think he is. He's fae, though. Magic fumes off of the stranger in a stench of deadly waves. The black robe skims over the dirty floor, picking up the ash and carrying it along with every hobbling step he takes. Ridges and bumps protrude from a smooth scalp. Worn skin sags against the angles of his face. Deeply etched lines cover his features. When he fully meets the dim light of the chandelier above our table, a gasp pulls from my lips.

Mangled and twisted skin is scarred over his eye sockets. Long, gnarled fingers bump unsteadily into the chairs as he feels his way closer to us.

"Traveler, we've been eager to introduce you to our new guest," the woman says, standing quickly from her seat. She rushes to his side, clinging to his frail arm and leading him to my side.

A thrashing feeling shakes through me as my heart pounds recklessly for me to take some form of action. From beneath the table, I slowly pull the knife from my boot. The warm blade skims up my calf and I grip it tightly as I stare up at the fae.

"Zakara, this is the Life Traveler. He is a seer who came to us years ago," the king says proudly.

A scoff is all that passes for a moment. Ryder's lips twist into a cruel smile as he stares hard at the glossy shine of the tabletop.

"Had he stayed in the Hopeless realm he would have been executed. Do not pretend he came to you of his own free will," Ryder says, glaring across the table at Tristan.

Heavy, rasping breaths shake from the Traveler's dry lips and he raises a single hand. A gray rotting color tones his flesh, and knobs of bone protrude from his arched fingers. My eyes close tightly as his fingertips meet my pale hair. A burning smell wafts through the air as the frayed edges of his heavy robes rub across my cheek. The closer he comes the stronger his magic feels. It strikes right into my body with stinging pain. It's a sweeping current of power that steals my breath away.

Then he's gasping with pain. My eyes fling open to find Darrio clasping the Traveler's thin wrist. Whisking white smoke fumes from Darrio's hand.

"Do not touch her." An unspoken threat blazes in his beautiful gaze and my chin rises a little higher as the Traveler lowers his hand. I don't know if I have an ally in Darrio but it does appear that way. And an appearance is all I have right now.

The metallic hilt of the knife cuts into my palm as I grip it tighter and finally stare up into the Traveler's face. His shoulders shake slightly and his eerie face tilts toward me. It's as if he can feel my gaze on his slick and scarred skin.

Who did this to this fae?

And more importantly, why?

The warmth of Darrio's palm slips over my knuckles as he pulls the knife from my hand.

When the Traveler opens his mouth, my skin crawls, wishing to inch away from this man who isn't a man at all. He's more of a shell of a life that's breathing down on me, drenching me with anxious nerves.

"I feel it in her," he says in a rattling voice that circles the room like a winter breeze. His head tips back as his body begins to tremble. "Power rages through her. I can see her clearly in my travels."

A scraping sound startles me from his coarse sounding words.

I glance to the head of the table and Tristan is standing now, staring down on me like I'm a fortune he can't afford to lose. Then I see it. A metallic glint at his waistband catches my eye and power definitely rages through me now.

Fury like I've never felt before stings my nerves, making my fists shake.

At his thin little hip sits my father's blade. My only inheritance I've ever had rests against his hip as if I didn't sail into this hellfire land with it in my hands.

"Three Hopeless will bring us our salvation.

The time has come, just as I said it would, my master." The way the Traveler says 'master' makes more anger flood my chest, but then he says something that halts everything. My whole world stops and comes crashing down when he says, "She is the salvation. She is the Eminence. I am sure of it."

All the anger in me drains at the sound of his words. My attention swings to the fae who brought me here. Ryder's shining blue eyes hold my gaze with a look of awe. His full lips part on a breath but no words come out.

Everyone stares down on me, their gazes feeling heavy on my slight shoulders. I can't seem to look away from Ryder or his gentle eyes. I can't even catch my breath so I just keep looking to him for some kind of assurance.

He's the type of person who could say anything and I'd believe it. There's a defined confidence in him that makes me believe every word he says.

I need him to say I'm not what they say I am. I need to hear him say it.

His quiet words don't bring me assurance, though.

"Shit. You're the Eminence."

Chapter Five
Chemistry

I'm not the Eminence. I don't think someone with that title is allowed to be as big of a fuck up as I am. There should be some requirements. Some sort of past experience. Eminent training of some sort involved. Eminence boot camp, maybe. My qualifications just aren't there. Maybe I'm just a temp.

Ryder's cryptic words from when we first met echo through my mind:

The Eminence is said to be the most powerful Hopeless in the entire world. Someday, the Eminence will come and it'll either rain wrath on this already demolished world, or it'll restore it to the beauty it once was.

A shaking breath leaves me as I reject the responsibility of that title.

Tomorrow. Tristan said we'd discuss my future tomorrow.

A stream of denial accompanies me all the way back to my room. My steps trail after Darrio's, one after the other in a nice repetitive form but that's all they are. My actions aren't thought out for once. I can't calculate anything around me. My mind is a stuttering carousel of one word and one word only: *Eminence*.

"Are you alright?" A voice like warm hot chocolate sinks right into me and brings my attention back into focus. I drag my gaze from the black dust coating the hall floor to heavy boots, fitted dark jeans over strong thighs, lean hips and a broad chest. Tendrils of a black beard shadow his strong jaw, a stark contrast to his pale, troubled eyes.

"Are you alright?" he asks once more and it's then that I realize we've stopped walking and he's opened my bedroom door. Daxdyn peeks up at us from his spot on the floor. He's slumped down at the foot of my bed and exhaustion lines his beautiful face.

"What's wrong, my pretty little human?" Darrio asks in a whisper. His eyes harden with concern and more hesitation than I've ever seen him hold. He slowly brings his hand to my hip. From that simple touch, tingles spread through me, right to my core. The warmth of his palm seeps right into my flesh, almost pushing out the building anxiety I've felt since the moment we stepped foot onto this hellish island.

His gray eyes are locked onto mine, and for a moment, I just stare at him. How did I ever let myself become so weak around Darrio? I hate the way it feels. I hate the way I want to just lean into him and let him take care of me.

No one takes care of me but me.

I almost consider lying to him. I could push a fake smile onto my lips and tell him everything's okay. I could easily say I'm just tired. I'm not feeling well. I'm fine.

But I can't. I don't want to. I don't want to lie to Darrio.

"If he believes I'm the—" It's hard for me to say the word out loud, but I force it out. "Eminence, he'll hurt me. He'll use me, Darrio. Do you understand that? Don't trust him."

Don't let him hurt me, I want to scream. But I don't. I won't. Asking Darrio not to trust him is the most I can manage.

How much of what Darrio's doing is an act and how much of it is real?

His head tilts a fraction, his eyes studying me and the minimal information I just gave him. An odd feeling of fear begins to trickle into me. What if Darrio doesn't care about who I trust and who I don't? My word means nothing in this kingdom.

The sweep of his thumb across the fabric of my dress, firmly over my lower hip bone, holds my attention. It sends goosebumps over my skin. With the smallest of movements, he traces circles over my hip as he appears to think.

Then he nods, just a short jarring of his head. "Okay."

"Okay?"

Again, he takes in every detail of my features.

"Okay. If you don't trust him, then neither do I. We just have to keep up an act for a little longer." The tone of his voice drops to a promising whisper. "I won't let him hurt you."

My heart melts; right through my chest. It's pooling into a pathetic, sappy puddle at this man's feet. All I want to do is throw my arms around him and wrap every inch of my body around every inch of his.

I smother the feeling out and cross my arms safely over my chest as I nod almost carelessly.

"Good."

A smirk pulls at the corner of his lip, making me want to kiss him there.

"Good."

And like two associates coming to a professional agreement, we end the conversation. It's ended with heated gazes and tingling feelings that I might never admit to.

Darrio glances back to Daxdyn and his lips pull into a low frown.

"Take care of my brother, okay?" The warmth of his body brushes against mine, his hard core lining up with my soft curves. He leans into me and I study his lips closely but he doesn't close that frustrating distance between us.

"I think Dax can take care of himself," I say.

That thin line that's covering his lips stays stern.

"Good night, Kara," he whispers, his big hand trailing across my abdomen as I walk into my room, leaving him in the dim hall.

The door pulls shut behind me and I listen intently for that little clicking sound of the lock turning in place.

An odd peace settles in me once I hear it. A sense of safety fills every fiber of my being from that tiny little sound.

The size of the room makes the man before me look insignificant. The balcony doors are still open, just as I left them hours ago. And, strangely, Daxdyn is still in his boxer briefs. His pale shoulders hang low as he sits on the dirty floor at the foot of my enormous bed.

Dark lashes flutter as his cloudy gray eyes meet mine. There's no happiness in them. His eyes hold an emptiness that I've never seen before.

Slowly I make my way toward him, lowering myself to my knees. The hard floor bites into my skin but I can't seem to notice anything but the look that's lining this man's beautiful face.

"Daxdyn, what are you doing?"

Did they do something to him?

Fear and anger burns through my tight chest.

If they hurt him, I'll kill them. I'll kill them all.

"I'm fine. Just tired," he whispers in a shaking voice.

His hand rises until his finger skims up the curve of my knee. His touch ignites that feeling all

63

through my body and I lean into him.

I don't believe a single word he just said, but I can't bring myself to contradict him.

So I don't say anything. The soft blankets meet my back as I slump down next to him. His arm slips over my shoulders and he holds me to him, his fingers trailing little paths along my skin. Gently his lips brush against my temple and my eyes close on contact.

I hold a breath within my lungs and I let the details of the night fall away as I bask in the faded calm that Dax gives me.

Some time passes before his fingers skim the underside of my thighs and he pulls me up to his chest. I settle into his body as he carries me to the soft bed. The warm blankets seclude us and his hard body never leaves me. We lie carefully side by side, his shoulder against mine, our thighs neatly touching.

The familiar smell of smoke clouds my thoughts as sleep begins to pull me under.

A strong arm pulls me against his side and I burrow my head into the nook of his shoulder. There's something about being manhandled in a bed that wakes up every part of your body. Energy swirls tightly in my core, sparking within me.

A comfortable silence passes and just when I'm about to drift to sleep again, he speaks.

"You know, you don't have to pretend like you haven't slept with Darrio."

My eyes fling open. It's like his empathic emotions can't feel the churning of awkwardness within me, as if that feeling has never existed in him in his entire life.

"What makes you think I have?"

His fingers begin to drift along my arm, sending goosebumps across my flesh.

"The chemistry between you two is almost combustible." His words aren't spoken with jealousy. It's just a statement to him, but it does seem to be something he's thought a lot about.

Chemistry? Is that what he's calling the love-hate tension Darrio and I have?

I don't even know how to respond, but I try.

"I wish I could explain it. Darrio isn't that terribly likable." And yet, he is in a way. My gaze meets his, finally; the pale light in the room seeps into his features, washing out his coloring.

Laughter rumbles through his chest, shaking into me until a smile pulls at my lips.

"That's what sucks about it. He's an asshole and still you're drawn to him. It really kills my ego, just so you know."

His tongue rolls across his bottom lip as he smirks down at me. His light eyes shine, making him impossibly sexier. I love his happiness and it soothes me just seeing his smile again.

"Aww, do you need me to stroke your ego, Dax?" My palm skims across the cut lines of his hard chest, tracing his pectorals with a daring finger.

"I don't need your pity strokes." His teeth sink into his lower lip as he bites back a smile. His heated eyes study my features, his gaze falling to my mouth before he pulls me closer and presses his lips to my hair once more.

Warmth spreads all through me and for an instant I hate myself for making our relationship harder than it has to be.

I should tell him he should leave. Our friendship feels shaky, like at any moment we both might teeter over the edge into something more sinfully complicated.

Neither of us speaks. We ignore the tension that fills my nerves. We ignore the way he makes my heart calm just from his presence.

We ignore every emotion that screams at me to be heard.

I need Daxdyn and I can't screw up any more than I already have.

Chapter Six

Freedom and Vengeance

Warmth surrounds me when I wake. My eyes refuse to open as I just settle into that content, calm, and safe feeling of comfort. My palm lightly traces the cut lines of Daxdyn's smooth abdomen and his hand is pressed to the center of my back, holding me against the side of his body.

Rough fingertips skim up and down my arm, making me crazy with the minimal contact.

"Wake up, my human," a deep voice whispers in a rumbling tone.

My lashes flutter and I glance up to see Daxdyn's serene face. His lashes shadow his high cheekbones and even breaths leave his parted lips.

He's still asleep.

Shit, he's still asleep.

My eyes widen as I turn in Daxdyn's arms to see Darrio resting with his back against the glossy headboard.

"Good morning." His dark brows raise but he doesn't say anything more.

This looks bad. I should explain. I should say something.

Nothing but heavy emptiness clouds my thoughts.

"He okay?" Darrio asks, nodding to his brother who's half-naked at my side.

That's what he cares about. He cares about his brother. The rage Darrio always seems to hold isn't in his eyes when he looks at his twin. Right now, all he has is … worry.

"He seems alright. He looked worn out last night." I pause trying to understand what I'm missing. "Why did Tristan refer to Dax as the aggressive one?"

Darrio's eyes flicker to the open balcony door. Warm water colors of pale orange and yellow splay through the dusty room. The light beams off the only clean surface; the bed frame.

"A story for another time, my human."

My eyes narrow on him but I let it go.

"Does he want to see me already? So early?" I turn; Daxdyn's hand rests against my stomach now as I face his brother.

Darrio sits with his long legs crossed, his dirty boots resting atop the twisted white sheets.

"No, no one's awake yet."

A line creases my brow as I stare up at him.

Footsteps fall heavy against the hardwood floors and I sit up slightly to see Ryder standing in the doorway. His brows rise as he looks at the three of us lying in the enormous bed.

For a second I consider telling him there's room for one more but I bite my sarcasm back.

"There are other mortal women, you know. You guys don't have to crowd just one." Ryder smirks at Darrio but he doesn't return the humor.

Damn it, I should have said it! The one time I try to be the adult in the room and I miss my moment to torment him.

"Are we ready or are you guys enjoying your stay here?" Ryder raises his hands impatiently from his sides.

"What is he talking about, Darrio?"

His big hand brushes over mine, tangling his fingers through mine before he says in a quiet voice, "I told you we weren't staying long."

An energy courses through my veins and I'm shoving out of the hot blankets within seconds. I crawl over Darrio's large frame, his legs tangling with mine as I stumble from the bed. Daxdyn sits up, probably awake from the commotion I'm causing. Squinting eyes follow my movements and he brushes his fingers across his beautiful but tired face.

My feet skim in a rush across the cold floor. Without embarrassment, I begin pulling on my torn jeans; my dress hides my ass for the most part. Daxdyn, Ryder, and Darrio don't look away. There's zero shame in the room and, apparently, none of us are afraid of my body. I face the wall as I tug the black dress over my head and begin buttoning up my vest with minimal privacy. My heavy boots are gathered up from the floor in an instant. I stumble a few times more as I tug them on and stagger toward the door.

"Are we fucking going or not?" I ask and they all three look at me like I'm a madwoman.

Daxdyn takes more time than I did to pull himself from the bed and dress. His wrinkled cotton shirt hugs his corded arms. I give him a

71

small smile but he only stares blankly at me. There's an emptiness in his bright eyes that cuts me deep.

Ryder watches his friend closely, his brows lowered with concern but he doesn't say a word.

"Alright, let's go." Darrio nods to Ryder as he clasps his brother's shoulder. Daxdyn's lean body wanes under the impact of Darrio's reassuring hand.

Ryder turns on his heels and looks down each hall before the four of us scurry from my room. The deeper into the castle we go, the more hesitant our steps become. When we hear footsteps, Ryder swing's his arm out, pressing me to the wall as we wait for the heavy sound to fade away. He nods and, oddly, his hand wraps around mine as he pulls me along. Warmth fills me from his hand on mine, but it doesn't stop my restless heart from trying to beat its way out of my chest.

We trail through the long, dark corridors on anxious steps for so long I begin to wonder if the former prince has forgotten his way through these halls.

He opens another door and the dense smell of smoke coats my lungs as the filtered morning sunlight warms my face.

The sun threatens the horizon but the cloudy smoke in the air veils its existence.

"Almost there," Ryder whispers, pulling me closer to him as we scale the stone wall of the castle. Our backs press flat against it, my boots scuffing over the stone with each step I take. Muddy grass coats our steps and I realize how easy it would be to track us.

"Where are we going?"

"We need to go to the Hopeless realm. We'll be safe there." Darrio's voice is only a whisper but it carries in the cool wind.

"*Safer*, you mean," Daxdyn adds from over my shoulder.

My stomach twists at the sound of his words.

What does he mean *safer*? As if the Hopeless realm has its own dangers I should be worried about.

Am I ready to go to the Hopeless realm? To change everything I've ever known about myself? What if I am the one the Traveler prophesied about? What if I am destined for greatness or destruction?

People know when they're important, don't

they?

I'd know if I were anything more than just a thief …

"What about my sword?" I ask in a quiet tone.

Ryder glances back at me, his brows lowering over his pale eyes.

"We can't get your sword, Kara. Tristan has it."

Ryder pulls his attention away from me to look around the corner of the castle.

"It was her father's," Daxdyn adds and it warms me in a strange way that he remembered that.

"Well do you want your sword, or do you want your freedom?" Ryder asks as if I'm being childish.

My shoulders square and annoyance stings through me.

"I want both," I say, anger tingeing my voice.

Ryder cocks a brow at me, but doesn't reply.

My jaw clenches shut as I realize these people have taken the last little piece of my father that I had left. Tristan is prancing around this kingdom with a sword he isn't good enough to hold.

Freedom. That's what I crave. I'll follow these fae. I'll claim my power, whatever power that might be, in the Hopeless realm.

And then I'll return for the sword my father left me as he died in these streets at the hands of a terrible queen.

Freedom and vengeance go hand in hand, after all.

Chapter Seven

The Eminence

Freedom isn't at all what we find when we turn the corner.

A tower reaches up high into the gray sky. Brick after brick is stacked until it shadows over our small bodies.

"What the hell is that?" Ryder asks.

Darrio runs his hand along the foundation. "Looks like their way of controlling the borders."

"They built a wall around the realm?" The line between Ryder's brows is severe as he stares in disgust at the soot staining the tan brick.

On careful steps, we trail the perimeter of the circular building. It isn't very large at all; the size of a room, maybe. But, once again, I'm very aware of the deep prints we're leaving behind us.

A single door faces the castle and I begin to turn on my heels to look up at the grand but deteriorating castle. Little black flags flap in the wind and I can almost make out a faded white emblem in the center of them. There are posts set up at every corner, but no guards are in sight.

"In or out, gentlemen. We can't linger out here," I tell them as my gaze searches manically for an unseen threat.

Ryder's hand grips the doorknob and he slowly turns it.

With ease, the door pushes open. The three men look at one another with pure hesitancy in their tense frames.

The door to the tower surrounding the Hopeless realm is carelessly unlocked.

This is bad.

This is a set up.

"You ever feel like everything we're doing is just one big shit show that someone else is directing?" I ask as my hand grips around the hilt of the knife at Darrio's side. Without asking, I pull it from his leather belt.

The three of them glance back at me but don't reply.

Darrio pushes at the side of the door and walks

like a predator into a den. I can't see around his large shoulders but bright light is shining past him. The golden color highlights his body as if he truly is a descendant of an angel.

A descendant of the God of War would be more accurate.

Ryder follows closely behind him and Daxdyn presses his warm hand to the small of my back. He seems to hover at my side, as if he's more concerned about me than anything that might be in this tower.

The hard handle of the knife presses into my palm as my fingers tighten around it.

My eyes squint from the harsh lighting, and it takes me a minute to really assess my surroundings.

A curved room spirals up into sky and the morning light filters into the wide opening at the top. Six spotlights shine down on the brick floor and what rests at the center has my fullest attention.

Every scar on my arm burns, tingling to life. I stare wide-eyed at the inky pool of water that swirls in a perfect circle at Ryder's feet.

He stares down at it, his head hung low. His

shoulders sag a little as well.

All three of them seem to have their strength falling from them as the look down at the black iron bars that are firmly drilled into the cement. The bars cross over the swirling waters. It's like a well that's been covered up with prison bars.

"That's it?"

That's the entrance to the Hopeless City?

Ryder nods but he doesn't look away from the imprisoned well. He kneels, his boots teetering against the bars. He shoves his hand through and it barely fits into the small square opening. His fingers cut through the waters and the black angles that scar his arm darken.

The mark of the Hopeless flares to life on contact with the water.

"They've closed it off from us? They knew we'd try to escape. They were just waiting for us to find this." Daxdyn's empty voice crawls through the room and I, too, feel my strength slip away from me.

There really isn't any hope left in this world.

There certainly isn't any for us.

"Did you know it's rude to come late to a celebration held in your honor?" Tristan's question holds pure condescending snark.

The four of us stand on the outskirts of a jostling room of people. Their flowing gowns dot the room in vibrant colors of red, green, blue, black and white. Each color is more lavish than the last.

And here I stand with torn jeans and fresh mud clinging to my scuffed boots.

Darrio led us here as quickly as possible.

We can't leave. There's nowhere for us to go. Ryder had told me, his warm hand tugged on mine, trying to lure me back into the castle we had just fled from.

And, like an idiot, I followed them. Because part of me knows they're right.

I am fae. I am the Eminence.

Or, at least that's what all these beautiful people want to believe.

A large woman in a tight dress leans into a man and holds her hand to her mouth as she whispers to him. Another person does the same. Then another, and another.

Until it's an overbearing crowd of scuttling

whispers.

The Eminence.

The rush of words turns into hissing sounds that sets my nerves on edge.

Daxdyn's hand brushes over mine and he leans into me. "It'll be okay," he tells me, his head lowering close to mine, his soft brown hair skimming my forehead.

A faded feeling of calm pushes at the edges of my emotions but the anxiety out climbs it.

Tristan looks from Dax to me but I don't give the judgmental king a second glance.

The whispers hush to a dull murmur as a shuffling figure appears on the oval stage at front of the room. Yellow lighting falls upon the figure, giving him a more sickly skin tone. The intricate golden trim of the room doesn't catch the dim lighting. The grandeur of this castle is wasted with minimal lighting and dirty windows.

But the lighting doesn't take away from the ominous presence of the Traveler. The ends of his dark cloak swish with every hobbling step he takes. Finally, his gnarled face looks sightlessly out at the horrified crowd who stares up at him.

"Our time has come, my children." The Traveler's voice crawls over us and I lean closer to Daxdyn's calming warmth. "My Eminence, please join me."

He can't see a thing.

I have to remind myself that he cannot see a thing.

But it doesn't stop him from skimming the crowd until his attention lands hard on me.

A chill scurries across my flesh, and I stiffen my spine against the fear that's growing within me.

The long length of his curved fingers reaches out to me, cryptically inviting me to join him where he stands.

What kind of power resides within the Traveler? I felt it when we met. It's a dark and chilling feeling that makes my skin crawl just thinking about it.

Two steps are all I manage to take before Daxdyn pulls me back to him. I look up at him, our eyes meeting as he searches my features.

Without a word, he kisses the top of my head before shoving me toward the stage.

I stagger, my boots scuffing the recently

polished floor. The white tile gleams beneath my dirty boots and I wonder if I'm leaving a nice trail of mud behind me.

The mass of people part for me. My bare shoulders brush against theirs minimally and my fingers rake across expensive gown after expensive gown. I make sure to keep my head held obnoxiously high as I walk among the people of this kingdom. I meet a few of their gazes, looking into their eyes with a tightly held jaw and a hard purse of my lips.

No pleasantries are offered to them.

They think I'm a person of amplified strength.

And so I will be.

I walk with confidence up the few curving steps that lead to the hunched over figure at the center of the stage.

In a strange world of Travelers and Eminent beings, who holds the higher authority? I quickly consider which of us is more important.

I am.

I am the all-important, all-seeing, all-saving Eminence.

But their Traveler brought me here to *my*

people.

With that thought, I give a swift nod of greeting before bowing ever so slightly. Loudly within my ears my heart pounds, but without hesitancy, I pick up the mangled hand he holds out to me. A tingling sensation courses into my fingers, hinting at the powers swirling within him. It's an electric feeling but it isn't as strong as it was when I first met him. It isn't alive like it was before.

My lips pull into a hard line, pushing back the vomit I feel burning up my throat. My breath catches as I decide to make my mark on these watchful eyes.

His skin is like holding cold, wet leather in my palm. Slowly I press my lips to his knuckles, my lashes fluttering up to meet the scarred flesh that's covering his eyes.

A collective gasp collides through the room and I smile to myself as I slowly rise from my position. Pure authority is all I hold in my swift movements.

"Traveler, thank you for bringing me to my people," I say in an airy voice of true entitlement. I look proudly down at each of their faces. I look at them as if they all hold a special place in my heart.

A special place in hell is more like it.

I note a few women close their eyes as their lips begin moving. It only takes a moment for me to realize they're praying. Their palms are held out to me, absorbing my presence, my words, and my unseen power.

I spot Darrio there in the crowd and he exchanges a smirking look with Ryder.

Did they doubt me for even an instant?

"Eminence, we've waited so long for you." The Traveler grips my hand tightly as if he's afraid I'll disappear right from this stage.

"You were not ready, my sweet servant." I'm summoning a goddess like persona. Suddenly my steps are lighter. Yes, my jeans are still tight and tattered but my goddess charisma is not.

From this distance, I can still see Darrio's eyes rolling at my dramatic antics.

Oh, ye asshole of little faith.

Jealous is what he is.

"Have your king remove our bindings and I will show you just how ready you all are." My voice carries over the crowd and I pause to meet Tristan's gaze.

If he removes their iron cuffs, any one of them will have the strength to tear the bars off of the Hopeless well.

Tristan's arms are folded across his black tuxedo. Not a crease or speck of ash blemishes his appearance. A charming smile pulls at his lips and slowly he lowers his power stance and makes his way toward the stage.

As he climbs the stairs, I extend my hand to him, inviting him into the shit show that I'm currently the main performer in.

His fingers lace through mine, and my skin crawls as he draws me closer to his feeble side. My thigh brushes against my father's sword hanging from his hip and it takes everything in me not to pull it from his belt and gut him on this stage.

A beautiful smile is all I give him.

The mass of people begins to fall to their knees, one by one. Urgent and wanting whispers fan through the room, suffocating me with every prayer that's spoken in my name. The forced happiness on my face falls slightly. A young woman walks slowly through the crowd and they part for her as if she, too, is of godly ranking.

She's a little younger than me, maybe twenty at the most. Glossy black curls hang loosely around her heart shaped face.

When I see her come to the front, my smile

slips away entirely into an honest look of fear.

In her small hands, she holds a large bowl and a short dagger. Unheard words skim across her full lips as she stares with intensity at me. That fear climbs through me, clawing up my lungs and throat as I hold her desperate gaze.

Without warning, she slices the blade across her palm. Droplets of dark blood bead into the bowl. Her index and middle finger swipe across the pooling blood and she drags them down the center of her face as her breathless chanting words become faster.

One hand, the one with the deep slice severing through it, is held out to me while the other grips that dagger a little tighter.

"In the name of the Eminence," she whispers like a vow just as she raises the dagger above her chest.

I fall hard to my knees, scuttling across the glossy floor until I'm on my hands and knees right in front of the young woman. My hand grips her shaking wrist as I hold her wild gaze. The bowl filled with her blood tips and a crimson color coats the stage like an extra layer of gloss. It slides warmly over my hand as I hold myself up in front of her.

"I am not a god," I say loudly for all to hear.

The dagger falls with a clattering sound to the floor and I can't bring myself to look away from the woman. I nod slowly at her until she mimics my nod of understanding.

"The Eminence is not a god," I repeat for good measure. "Sacrifices are not to be made in the name of," I pause, the words *false prophet* feeling thick on my tongue, "fae. Fae are not gods. Do you all understand?" It's then that I pull my hard gaze to the mass of adoring mortals.

Their eyes hold a look of confusion but they nod anyway.

"My Eminence," the Traveler says, pulling me from my dark thoughts. His feeble hand grips mine and he pulls me to my feet. His cold hand continues to hold mine as he brings it to his lips. Dry, cracking lips rake over my knuckles and that smile presses tighter against my teeth as I beam up at him with renewed, but waning, confidence. "We are ready for you, but you are not ready."

That smile pulls from my face as his words sink in. Circling whispers grow through the crowd.

"Not today," I say as if we're both on the same page. Swiftly, I push that false happiness back into place. My hand clasps his as he still clings to my other.

"I am much too tired today." I drop his hand and, without another word, I push past him.

He releases me with ease but I feel his attention burning a hole through my back. It only fuels my confidence as I take my place back by my men.

My men.

If, for the rest of my life, everything I ever do is all an act, I can at least rest assured that these men are mine. These people here today don't know what real loyalty is.

But I do.

They didn't imprison me; they're trying to save me. They're trying to rescue me just like I rescued them.

Tristan smiles and gives a small wave to his people before trailing after me. He joins us, his wife scurrying over to his side. Her white gown clings too tightly to her overflowing chest. A needy look is all she possesses as she waits patiently at Tristan's side, but his eyes are fully focused on me.

It doesn't take long for her neglected attention to shift.

Queen Anna's gaze settles darkly on Ryder and he holds her stare for several seconds.

What's flashing through his mind right now?

Judging by the look of hate in his narrowed eyes and the hard set of his jaw, I'd say a fine mixture of anger and embarrassment.

Embarrassment sometimes fuels anger. The stupidity you feel from letting your emotions turn you into something weak is a match for the fires of rage.

My fingers drift to his arm, pulling his attention to me. We both ignore the dry blood that coats my fingertips. A line creases his brow as he looks down on that small touch.

"Will you dance with me?" I ask in a shy whisper. With intent, I arch my back ever so slightly until my chest is pushing against his arm.

Curious confusion is all he has in his eyes. His blonde brow rises but he nods anyway.

His warm hand slips down until our fingers our interlocked and he walks me to the center of the room. I feel her attention on us, stabbing right through me. Dancers sway past us. Beautiful gowns of every color swish by, led by crisp-suited men.

Stiffly he holds my hips and I lock my hands lazily behind his neck. There's enough space between us to invite Daxdyn and Darrio over as well but I don't think Ryder would appreciate that thought.

The space of the grand room brings back memories. It's a public space, parties and announcements are held here. I've been here a few times before, years ago.

I swallow hard at the thought.

"What are you doing, beautiful?" he asks in a hushed tone, his light eyes sweeping over the busy room like he's waiting for a trap I've somehow set up in my free time.

"I just thought ..." I bite the inside of my cheek and consider the best way to phrase this. "I thought you'd want to make Anna jealous."

Laughter rumbles through his broad chest.

"I'm not a child, Kara. I don't have to go out of my way to hurt someone."

I think about how he spoke of a girlfriend when we almost kissed at my aunt's house.

"Why did you call her your girlfriend?" I ask as my fingers begin to toy with the shaved sides of his blonde hair. I don't know why it makes me happy that he's no longer with her. It's a petty and strange feeling.

Lightly his fingers push against my jeans, skimming over my bare hips just slightly.

"Like my brother said, she was a pawn to him. I didn't love her but I think everyone deserves closure. Maybe she knew his plans and maybe she didn't."

"I think she did," I say, making him smirk down at me.

His shifting eyes rake over me, drifting down to my lips and then further down to my chest. I feel his attention skimming across my flesh like a light touch.

"If I wanted to make someone jealous, what would you suggest?"

A smile curves my lips as I lead us into a smooth dance across the floor. He lets me; he lets me guide our graceful steps.

I move just as I did when I was a young girl in dance class. I move like a refined lady instead of a dangerous thief.

"Well, for starters, I'd think you'd want to

eliminate this space that's preventing the feel of my body pressing perfectly against yours."

Without another word, his hands dip low on my back, pulling me close against his hard chest. I watch the sharp angle of his Adam's apple as he visibly swallows.

My heart pounds against his chest, racing his heartbeat to an end that I'm not sure either of us is ready for.

"Then what?"

We're moving slower now, just the two of us swaying as our hips shift against one another.

"Then I think you'd lean in and whisper something witty in my ear and I'd laugh prettily as I pretend it's the most charming thing I've ever heard."

His lips are close to mine and they skim across my jaw as his head dips low. Warm breaths shiver across my neck and every nerve in my body waits for whatever it is he might whisper in my ear.

My breath catches as his lips press against the corner of my jaw, just near my ear.

"Like this?" The rasping of his voice has my body melding into his and I nod without thought as my eyes flutter closed. "Kara?" he asks, his lips brushing against the shell of my ear in a warm, breathy tone.

"Yeah?" I ask as I arch into him.

"You're not laughing as if I'm the wittiest man you've ever heard."

"Hmm," a smirk curves my lips and I lean into him on the tips of my boots. In a quiet voice, I whisper, "Perhaps even I am not that good of an actress, my Prince."

A real laugh tumbles through him and I'm not sure if either of us is pretending anything for anyone right now.

"Careful, calling me a prince is grounds for treason."

I pull back slightly from him and it isn't Anna I search out in the crowd.

It's Daxdyn and Darrio.

Their height towers over the others and for an instant I panic as I wonder what Ryder and I really look like together.

It feels strange but I care what they think of me.

It's the first time in years that I care about what

someone thinks of me. There isn't anger in Darrio, or jealousy. Just ... concern. Silver eyes trail over every detail of the crowd, over every swaying body and he lands on me continuously. It's as if I'm the concern. I'm what's worrying this beautiful fae. Daxdyn's tired eyes stare off in the distance, not fixated on anything in particular.

"Then I think we should probably stop before we both lose our heads," I tell Ryder.

"My brother would like nothing more." The smile tilting his lips is charming. White and straight. Perfect.

I nod and step back from him. His hand stays laced in mine as he leads me back to Daxdyn and Darrio.

Tristan's calculating attention drifts from Ryder's hand on mine to Darrio who's staring down at me with heated attention.

Daxdyn pulls Ryder's arm and the two of them begin whispering among themselves as they walk toward the wine table. Ryder peeks back at me as he speaks to his friend and a knowing smirk tilts Daxdyn's lips at whatever was just said.

I can't help but wonder what they're whispering about.

Darrio takes a single step closer to me, his body breeding warmth into mine.

I want to lean into him. I want to let this shitty day fade away as Darrio holds me to his chest.

"Are you toying with all three of them?" Tristan's voice cuts through, interrupting my thoughts, but I continue to stare ahead, ignoring the high King of Juvar. "Even the unfortunate looking one?"

My spine stiffens as he nods to Darrio. The fae clears his throat before looking toward the lines of the white tile floor.

The unfortunate looking one?

The scar slicing down Darrio's face demands my attention, the slight tilt of his nose, the dark brows that are lowered over shining, serious eyes.

Then I think about how his perfect smile transforms his whole appearance. The strong body he carries with confidence and the loyalty he's shown me pulls to the front of my thoughts. In a way, I love every one of the twisting scars that line his hard body. They're an art that displays his resilience. He's a warrior through and through.

He's everything King Tristan will never be.

I tip my head up at the king, finally giving him my attention. My long blonde hair sways with the swift movement of my anger.

"Actually, the only thing unfortunate about Darrio is his personality."

A cough that sounds suspiciously like a laugh shakes through Darrio.

"You're an asshole," he whispers under his breath before taking a long drink of wine.

Tristan looks from me to Darrio and then back again.

"All three of them. You truly are a sorceress, Zakara"

I begin to nod even though I desperately want to roll my eyes at him.

"Yes, my vagina is quite the enchantress." My jaw snaps shut as I stare at the soot staining the wall behind him.

His look turns sour as his blazing gaze narrows on me.

"You're a crude little piece of fae trash."

It's suddenly hard to swallow. A hundred words threaten to vomit from my throat, but I force them back down. This is a dangerous kingdom. My words don't belong to me here. Tristan owns even my words and I'll choke them down if I know what's good for me.

"I'm not feeling well. If you'll excuse me." The sweetest of smiles press tightly to my lips.

A single step is all I take.

Thin fingers wrap around my upper arm until pain shoots through me. My jaw clamps tightly closed and I raise my glare to meet the king's hard gaze.

"You leave when I say you leave, Miss Storm." The cruel smile he gives me reminds me to keep my own pretend happiness in place across my lips.

Of all the words he just said, the word *Miss* burns through my mind on repeat. It's a formality that thieves like me aren't given. I haven't been a 'miss' anything in over five years. Because of his mother.

My jaw tics as I stare at the glossy tiles.

Darrio's wide shoulders bump mine as he shifts on his feet. His body interferes with the grip Tristan has on me. The king releases me as the two study one another. Fury burns through Darrio's smoky eyes like a fire that not even their iron shackle can put out.

"Do. Not. Touch. Her." His tone is a low sound of rasping rage. "She isn't one of your belongings." Darrio's deep voice vibrates through my own body, sending a shiver over my skin. His spine is ramrod straight and a false smile is held on his lips. It's more of a daring sneer really. His eyes are that steely gray color he always reserved for me when we first met. The king appraises Darrio's height, every strong muscled piece of him. Darrio's like a scarred weapon: dangerous and powerful.

The king's throat bobs. He curtly turns his back on both of us.

"Good night, Miss Storm."

Chapter Eight

Just a Kiss

"My personality is really unfortunate, is it?" Darrio's hard body cages me and a taunting smile tilts the corner of his lips. My bedroom door sways closed behind him.

One step after another and he has me pinned against my bedroom wall and it's all I can manage to just nod at him. My thighs shift as heat pools between my legs.

Warm hands push against my hips before meeting the bare skin of my ribs. A shiver shakes through me, and I tip my head up at him.

"Thank you," I whisper, the emotions in me crowding my thoughts.

"For what?"

"For demanding the king to see me as a real person and not just a possession."

I lean my head into the crook of his neck,

resting on him and hiding my face from the honesty I just spoke.

He cradles my body against his. His strong arms wrap around me with the full force of safety surrounding me.

"No one owns you, Kara." The warm, smooth tone of his comforting words tightens the feeling that's coiling within me.

I lean up on the teetering tips of my boots and press a soft kiss to his neck. I pause as he tenses beneath me but I don't let him speak before my tongue slips between my lips and I kiss there once more. Big hands skim down my body. He grips my ass hard as he holds me against him.

His beard scrapes my cheek as I rake my teeth across the sensitive skin of his neck and collar bone.

"Kara—" His rasping voice shakes through me and my hands twist into his hair. "I can't hurt Dax."

The sound of his brother's name is painful on his lips. It causes me to stop, halting every lust-filled thought in my head.

"What?" I ask on an empty breath. My chest pushes against his as I arch back to stare up at him.

The look in his eyes is confused and regretful.

"I won't hurt him. He likes you and I won't hurt him. I'm—I'm sorry." His hands move slowly from the curve of my ass to an almost platonic place on my hips.

"I wouldn't hurt him either." My brows pull together as we both stare at each other in silence.

"Good." He nods continuously. "Good. You'd be good for him."

That word is repeated so much that it's swimming through my mind.

Good.

"What you and I have isn't good?" I ask so quietly it hurts my chest to whisper it.

His brows raise high toward the dark locks that are loose around his face.

"What we have is ... more than good."

My hand drifts from the base of his neck to the coarse stubble along his jaw. My thumb rakes over his beard before skimming his lower lip.

He never kissed me.

Not really.

Not since I slapped the hell out of him that first time.

Why didn't he ever kiss me?

All the moments we've shared feel wasted now because of the loss of a kiss that we never got to have.

I'll never get to know what it'd feel like to let him care about me. Somehow, he's lowered my walls and just when I'm defenseless he's turning away, leaving me open and wounded for just anyone to see the damage I'm hiding within.

"Kiss me." It's a torturous sound that leaves my lips. A pleading request that I can feel aching within my chest.

His warm hand slides up my forearm before clasping around my knuckles. He pulls my hand back, away from his mouth and he stares down at me in silence for so long I'm sure he's about to walk away.

Slowly his head tilts closer and his temple leans against mine. My breaths are unstable and clash against his, drawing out this painful rejection that I feel coming.

"Close your eyes." The warm tumbling sound of his voice washes over me and I do as I'm told.

"No one's ever asked me to kiss them before," he says in a confessional whisper. "Have you thought about it a lot? Us kissing?" The warmth of his breath fans across my lips, but I can't tell if he's any closer or not.

The rough pads of his fingers skim along my jaw, chasing a shiver across my flesh.

I nod, still not opening my eyes.

"Hmm, so have I." Soft lips brush against the column of my neck followed by the tingling of his beard and my head tilts for him. His confession makes me realize how gentle he's been with me, how sweet he's been recently. "I've thought about it every day." A breath that sounds a little like a moan shakes through me as the warmth of his tongue sweeps over my jaw line as he kisses me there. "Every day since you let me fuck you." At that I do moan, my legs shaking as his body pins me to the wall. His hard length pressing just above my hips has me shifting against him. "Why'd you let me fuck you, Kara?" His mouth skims the corner of my mouth.

My lashes flutter open and with the nearly nonexistent space separating our lips, I consider his odd question.

"Because we're *exactly* the same. And there

isn't a single hurtful word you could say to me that could make me ignore the spark I feel when you're near."

A half breath is all he gives me before his lips slam onto mine.

His head dips low as his teeth rake across my lower lip, making me gasp long enough for his tongue to slip in. Pain and pleasure pulses through me as his nails dig into my skin and he grinds his hips in rhythm with mine.

With a rush of need my hands shove down his hard chest to the straining bulge in his jeans. My fingers fumble with the metal zipper for only a second before he's shoving them away and unzipping it himself. The smooth length of his dick meets my palm, making me wet at just the feel of his hardness.

Then his fingers are drifting over my lower stomach and he pushes my jeans down without bothering with the button. I teeter on my feet as I kick the clothes off. The distinct sound of a new tear in my jeans emits through the room but I don't dwell on it.

The stiff feel of him has my hand working quicker over his cock and he groans into my mouth. It's a sound that has me mimicking the vibrations of it. It's a sound that causes a soaring high to rocket through me, sending my emotions into a frenzy of unintelligible, lust-filled thoughts.

Until he grips my hips and flips me. In an instant, the cool wall is pressed against my cheek; the feel of his warm mouth is torn away from me as he holds my hips steady. Before I can even understand what's happening, the smooth head of his dick pushes at my entrance.

My lips part as I realize we're once again in the same setting as the first time we had sex.

"Darrio." My tone is quiet but it seems to command him at once. He stops where he is just behind me, straining against me. My hands are flat against the wall, my messy hair veiling my face from him.

"Yeah?" Heavy, shaking breaths fall against the back of my neck.

A few seconds pass as I consider my words carefully.

"Do you always have sex like this?" The tight grip he has on my hips loosens as if he might let go entirely.

I turn slowly and face him, my hands lingering against the swirling, inky lines peeking out along the base of his neck.

"I—" He swallows and then nods without adding to the confirmation.

My heart hurts a little as I think about the reasons he would have for preferring that position. The pink scar that lines his face meets my index finger, skimming down until the coarse feel of his beard drags over my skin. The slight tilt of his nose catches my attention, but his beautiful lips are more demanding. Every one of his imperfections is laid out for everyone to judge and I didn't think he gave two shits about their judgement.

But maybe he does.

"I want to see you, Darrio." I don't say it, but he's sexy. In a carnal way. I want to see what he looks like in the most carnal of moments.

He shakes his head no, rejecting my request without explanation.

He wants to play hardball?

Fine.

I can play hardball.

My body brushes every inch of his, including the hard length that's perfectly pressed low against my stomach. My lips skim his but only barely.

"I want to watch you." My lashes flutter up to watch him closely. "I want to watch you fuck me." That magic that always burns through him flashes in his silver eyes. I bite his lip before sucking lightly and then finally kissing it. "I want to watch you make me come." A groan vibrates through his chest and into mine.

"Fucking human," he says on a low, taunting voice.

Gently, he kisses me. His tongue makes slow work of flicking against mine. Darrio kisses me like he never wants to stop.

A girlish squeal tumbles from me when his strong hands grip the underside of my thighs and he pins me against the wall with nothing but his body and the castle walls holding me to this world.

And for once, I want to be here. He makes this hellish world tolerable.

Nice even.

Then he slams into me hard. My lips part with a harsh gasp and I hold his gaze as he drags his length slowly out before slamming into me once more.

Sharp edges of my nails rake up his tense back and swiftly I pull off his shirt so his warm skin pushes against mine. My fingers tangle into his lengthy hair and I pull slightly. A shiver runs through me as he rakes his teeth along the base of my jaw. A mixture of soft lips and biting teeth skim down my neck and shoulder.

I feel the coiling energy tighten recklessly, ready to explode.

Then my moans are drifting up the high arches of the ceiling, circling the room. I feel myself tighten around him with a shaking orgasm but it doesn't slow him down. It only seems to increase his pace.

Another shaking buildup of energy furls low within me, my thighs clenching around his lean hips. Sweat dampens our skin but it doesn't stop the friction of our bodies. He uses that friction, rubbing his shaft against me just right until I'm screaming all over again.

A primal growl leaves his lips, humming against my neck.

He doesn't stop until I'm clinging like a second layer to his strong and relentless body; the body that's strung tight beneath my touch. A low, long groan escapes him as he stills against me, burying his face into my messy, damp hair.

My fingertips trace the lines of hard muscle tone and jagged scars along his shoulders.

Hot breaths shake over my neck and neither of us speaks for several minutes.

Gently, his mouth presses to the thin scar that lines the base of my neck and he holds me against him. Black jeans are still wound around his feet as he carries me on unsteady steps to my bed. My legs feel weak as the soft mattress meets my tired limbs.

My knees curl up to my chest as I look into his shifting, avoiding eyes.

Silence. Silence clings to us as if we'll never have another word to speak to one another for the rest of our long, regrettable lives.

He bends and his jeans drag back up his thighs, covering himself once more. The amount of attention he gives the silver button on his jeans is suffocating. I can practically feel his heavy thoughts drifting in an unspoken voice through the quiet tension in the room.

The muscles of his arms ripple with the simple task of zipping his jeans. The black ink adorning the pale lines of scars across his shoulders shift with each move.

And I study his every detail.

I'm afraid I'll never get the unfiltered chance to look at this beautiful man like this again. My heart pounds with the terror that I'll have to avoid his starlight eyes, his rumbling voice, the alluring energy that he always pushes into me.

I swallow hard and try to steady the breaths that are wracking through my lungs.

Still he stares at the soot lining the floor.

He's going to say this was a mistake, I can tell.

The two of us are letting the silence smother the life out of us.

And it is. I feel it shoving against my chest, clutching ahold of my heart with each passing second.

"You going to scoot over or are you as big of a bed hog as you are a pain in my ass?" His attention drags from the floor to look me right in the eye.

My lips part as I stare wide-eyed at him. I clamp my jaw shut. The mound of blankets shifts until they're nearly falling off the bed as I scramble to make space for Darrio's large frame.

I kneel there at the edge, my gaze trailing his every step; waiting for him to join me.

And to my surprise, the fae lies down. He lies

down as if it's the only place he wants to be.

Stiffly he crosses his legs; one ankle over the other, his hands folded over his taut abdomen. At his side, I lie flat on my back and the two of us stare up at the swirling textured ceiling.

It's as if neither of us is sure how our bodies fit together, when they interlocked perfect just moments ago.

A beat passes, before the bed sinks and he curls his body around mine, his arm wrapping protectively across my stomach. His scarred skin skims over my smooth abdomen and he pulls my back tightly to his chest.

It takes a few seconds before his body actually relaxes against me. It's like he isn't used to holding someone but it feels good.

He feels good.

Not another word is spoken, but an insurmountable amount of emotions swirl around us both as we drift peacefully to sleep.

Chapter Nine
The Other Brother

Darkness meets my sight as the burning smell of ash floods my senses. The cool night air meets my lungs in waves.

Without disturbing the blankets, Daxdyn sits at the very edge of the mattress. His smoky eyes drift over my body and his brother's arm lying over my abdomen. There's no pull to his lips, just a straight line of blank emotions is all he gives me.

Once again, words fail me.

His long fingers push across the sheets until his fingers interlace with mine. The smooth pads of his fingertips toy with mine and he watches our hands intently.

"Are you okay, Dax?" I whisper so quietly it's hard for even me to hear my words.

A sinking sadness drowns within my chest and I can't explain the feeling. It's a crushing feeling that seems to dart out from the depths of my existence.

But then I realize my existence isn't its source at all.

It's his feelings.

It's Daxdyn's.

"Are you okay?" I ask again in a louder tone.

His lips part as his attention sweeps over the darkness that secludes us. The pale light of the moon tries to shine past the heavy clouds, but only a diluted shade of color slips into the room. The light gives Daxdyn's smooth skin a sickly hue that sinks into his strong bone structure, turning the sharp angles into sunken features.

"The iron traps our powers within us." A hollow sound follows his voice, an echo, a shadow of his feelings. "My powers are emotions. And my emotions are empty without the feel of others."

Nothing but the sound of his shallow breaths fills the silence as I think about what he's saying.

"Come here," I say, pulling at his hand until his head is lying on my hip. "Can you feel me?" His shaggy dark hair meets my fingers as I push his soft locks back from his face.

"A little. I feel your tension. Some emotions

are stronger than others, but the iron mutes everything." A deep breath shakes through him like he can't find a single breath to fill his lungs. I place one of my palms over his heart while my other continues to run through his hair.

An hour passes like that; me trying to push away the terrible feeling that I can sense coming off of him in drowning waves. Then he turns on his side, his face burrowing into the curve between my hip and ribs. His warm, even breaths fan across my skin, next to Darrio's big hand and I know he's finally fallen asleep. My fingers squeeze his while my other hand stays tangled in his dark locks.

"I love how much you care. Even when you try to pretend you don't," Darrio says in a low whisper that fans over my neck. His voice startles me and comforts me all at once.

Darrio's strong body is still spooned against mine, his hot flesh brushing against my spine with every rise and fall of his chest.

I'm a prisoner here. For the first time in my life, my life is not my own.

And all I can seem to think about is these two fae men.

Chapter Ten
Friends

"You three seem to be really shook up over the fate of our lives." Ryder's annoyingly condescending voice greets me first thing in the morning.

Soft hair is still threaded through my fingers and I untangle my hand from Daxdyn's hair. I push my palms across my face, trying to push aside how tired I still am and how sore I feel from my time with Darrio.

My legs clench closed, a soreness clings to my muscles and limbs.

I glance to him and Darrio looks at me with a small smile curving his lips before sitting up. The blankets pool around our hips and I still haven't even looked Ryder's way to give him the time of day.

"I didn't know sharing was your thing, Darrio." Ryder says with a tone filled with ridicule.

"It isn't what it looks like," I finally mumble,

sitting up.

Long blonde hair tangles around my face in knots of disheveled waves. My vest is askew and I quickly tug it back into place.

"Not what it looks like?" he repeats as his pale blue eyes shift from Darrio, to me, to Daxdyn.

Daxdyn glances up at me, a thin line set hard across his lips. He doesn't sit up. He doesn't appear to care at all what this day might hold. Long dark lashes shadow across his cheeks as he closes his eyes and rolls over, giving Ryder the span of his back.

"Whatever. You guys going to start the day or what? It's almost noon and I can't hide in my room any longer." Ryder's big hands shove into the pockets of his tight black jeans.

An impatient second passes while my legs shift beneath the blankets.

"Are you getting up, your Eminence?" He cocks a brow at me, nothing but snarky attitude is all he holds for me.

"I—" I bite the inside of my cheek as I remember how I just told him that this wasn't what it looks like …

"You what?" His arms rise from his sides, and he's all but tapping his muddy boot at me with childish irritation. "Spit it out."

"I'm not wearing any pants," I blurt in a screeching confession.

Darrio closes his eyes as if he can just disappear from this conversation. At the moment, I, too, am wishing I had that ability.

Ryder's judging gaze widens. Only a second passes before he turns on his heels and walks out, slamming the door behind him.

Is he annoyed, or is it possible my prince is jealous?

"I have to go," Darrio says. He crawls on his hands and knees across the tangled sheets until he's right in front of me. A surprise gasp parts my lips as his mouth presses to mine. With a quick flick of his tongue, he leaves me hungry for more, heat pooling between my thighs.

But he pulls back just as quickly as he came.

"Wait." My stomach turns as I realize what I'm about to say to him.

He pauses there, leaning toward me. The muscular lines of his chest threaten to distract me but only for a moment. Several seconds pass as he waits for me to say what's stuck in my throat.

"What is it?" His palm sweeps over the back of my hand.

"I need you to get me something." My gaze is locked on the way he's holding my hand, avoiding his confused look.

"What is it, Kara?"

My teeth sink into my cheek as I try to phrase this the best way possible.

"There's a plant called Silphium. Can you find a way to get it for me?" I don't expand on the request but I do finally look up at him.

This is the second time I've had sex in a two week time period. I need that plant. As much as the king likes me, I don't think he'd be pleased to see his honorable Eminence walking around the castle hormonal and pregnant.

Daxdyn shifts beneath the blankets but my attention is held on the look that's consuming Darrio. His lips part but he doesn't immediately speak. He blinks a few times while he looks at me and it almost looks like it hurts him to say what he's thinking.

"Kara, fire fae … the men … they can't …" He pauses one more time as he leans in close to me. "Fire fae can't reproduce." My stomach sinks as I study the line creasing his brow, the cracking sound of his confession. "My body heat burns too high."

"Oh," I say in an empty voice.

If I didn't know any better, I'd think the ever-aggressive fae is holding nothing but sadness in his downcast eyes.

"How old are you, Darrio?" I ask, sitting up on my knees, closing the space between us. His eyes slowly travel south and his tongue rolls against his lips before he meets my gaze again. My palms run through his beard, clasping his face in my hands. His palm skims over my knuckles.

"Almost two hundred."

"Two hundred?" I ask quietly.

Again, Daxdyn, shifts from behind me like the third wheel in this strange relationship.

"Give or take a decade, yeah."

I nod as I study his features.

He's two hundred years old and he'll never have kids. You probably have plenty of time to think about life when you've seen two hundred years pass you by.

"I have to go," he says again but in an empty voice this time.

"Okay." I nod and my lips gently press against his. Sweetly, he kisses me back, one hand held on mine and the other pushing low down my back.

"Stop worrying about me," he mumbles against my lips before pulling away. "And for gods' sake, put your pants on."

I smirk at his words.

He looks to his twin as he crosses the room. Sadness so deep it feels endless is held in his stormy eyes. His jaw tightens with a tic as he seems to recompose himself. Swiftly he pulls on his shirt before grabbing my jeans from off the floor and tosses them to me on the bed but he only half looks my way. One hand shoves through his long hair, pushing back what he might be feeling just as he opens the door to the stage that's becoming his new life.

When he closes the door behind him, I realize it's just Dax and I.

The cool sheets shift beneath me as I wiggle down until I'm pressed against his back. My arms wrap around his body. I once thought his body was solid muscle and pure strength. He doesn't feel that way right now. He feels like a shadow of the alluring fae I first met.

"You can go, Kara. You don't have to worry about me." He doesn't acknowledge the way I'm tangled around him. It's like my nearly naked body isn't there at all.

Gods above, let me help him. How do I help him?

"I'm not going anywhere." My voice whispers across his neck.

I don't know why, but I just can't help it; I press my lips there, to the shallow curve of his neck. Light stubble scrapes my lips. The start of a beard shadows his jawline and he slowly turns to me.

My heart stumbles when I see his gray eyes dilate. It's an angst-filled look that shines in his beautiful eyes and I can't seem to look away.

Soft lips skim lightly over mine, and a feeling that I've held deep within myself ignites with pent up vengeance. Once, twice, three times he presses his lips to mine, building that wanting feeling with every brush of his lips. I'm leaning into him, my blonde hair veiling our faces.

When he pulls back, a breath shakes out of him as he looks at me with life beaming within his features.

My lips part as I stare at him. Dax and I are friends. Weird, weird friends.

Right now we don't feel like friends.

"Good. Me either," he says with half smile.

Then he rolls over, snuggling back into the soft blankets as if he didn't just change the way I look at him.

***

A week passes like that; Dax and I curled up on the big bed. We keep ourselves entertained while we're locked away as the most luxurious prisoners I've ever seen.

He shoves another cookie into his mouth, practically swallowing it down in a single bite. The way his jaw moves as he eats is captivating my attention.

"Never have I ever ..." His bored tone drowns out as he thinks hard.

This has to be our hundredth round of never

have I ever. We're slowly running out of shocking confessions for the game.

"Never have I ever done anal with a nix during a blood moon."

I tilt my head at him slowly, his jaw tips up as he stares at the ceiling. For a few seconds, I just try to process what he said, my mouth opening without words.

He seems oblivious to my disturbed look.

"That's ... oddly specific."

What the hell is a nix?

His bare shoulders shrug against the white sheets, his arm brushing mine.

"I'm just telling the truth, Kara. Don't be ashamed if you have. There's no judgement in this game. I wouldn't judge you." He smirks, his lips curving up in a smile that has my heart stuttering.

We haven't kissed again. We've fallen back into a sense of normalcy. Just two comfortable friends who spend an obscene amount of time together with minimal clothes on.

Totally normal.

"Yeah, I haven't done that stuff either," I say

with confusion.

"Your tone doesn't sound too believable."

My eyes narrow on him even more.

Asshole.

I shove at his shoulder and he shoves back. His warm palm lingers against my skin long enough for my stumbling heart to notice. I push his bicep once more but he catches my wrist and I wiggle against his strong body. The two of us fuss like that for a few seconds until he grips both of my wrists, pinning my arms above my head in an instant.

My breath catches. A reckless feeling trembles through me as his strong body covers mine.

Our breaths mix between us as we stare with heated gazes at one another.

The sound of the door creaking open relaxes his hold on my hands but neither of us move.

"He wants to see you, Kara," Darrio's voice calls out to me and I shift until I'm sitting up. Dax lies back in his lazy spot once more.

"What does he want?" I whisper.

Darrio shifts on his feet but only shrugs.

"He said he wanted a meeting with his Eminence."

Perfect.

Chapter Eleven
Thieving Eminence

I'm distracted and tired and not at all prepared for whatever parlor trick the king is about to demand of me.

A toxic sort of tension fills the span of the large dining hall. The tabletop gleams with a fresh polish while the gray tiles have a new coat of ash lining them. Dim sunlight shines across Tristan's inky hair and he sits at the head of the table with his eyes fixated on me.

Darrio's shoulder brushes mine as he stands on my right-hand side and Ryder stands on my left. I'm a prisoner encompassed in power.

Anna hasn't looked up from her wine glass to acknowledge us. I assume it's intentional based on how much attention her husband's sending our way.

And to the king's right sits his mother. Her shining pink lips tip up in a smile and her hazy eyes spotlight only me.

"I knew my son would bring you to me." She nods with excitement and scurries from her seat.

"Step son," Ryder corrects in a lazy tone.

Her attention shifts over him for less than a second before deterring back to me. A shining color gleams in her eyes as she looks up at me in awe. Only a foot of space separates this regal woman from me.

Does she remember me? Does she remember murdering my father right in front of me? Does she know how often I imagine her death with vivid detail?

"We haven't been formally introduced." Less than a second passes before she speaks again. "Can I hug you, your Eminence?" Her voice is quiet and unsure but her eyes are big with excitement.

She wants to hug me? She trusts me to not rattle the life out of her elderly frame?

"Of course," I say with the breathy tone I imagine a serene deity might possess.

Her hands wrap around me and my shoulders stiffen on contact. My arms fold around her and my palm clasps against her neck. The delicate bones of her spine are apparent against my fingertips. A thin gold chain brushes over my palm and how simple it would be to snap her perfectly held neck flashes through my mind.

As she pulls back, I bring my hands firmly behind my back, squaring my posture. Nothing but an amazed smile is all she gives me.

"You're just as I expected you would be."

My hair is a tangled mess that desperately needs a real brush. My clothes are stained and unwashed. A shitty attitude is all I want to offer these people.

And yet, she stares at me with pride and adoration.

She's in for a disappointment.

"I've thought about it and I will release your binds." Tristan folds his pale fingers atop the table and my gaze drags to his slight frame. "But, only yours and only after I have your word you will restore this kingdom."

This kingdom.

Not the world.

This kingdom.

My lips pull together as I pretend to consider his offer.

Removing my cuffs won't do him a damn bit of good. Realistically it doesn't do me any good either …

Utter disappointment, I tell you.

He's clearly not stupid enough to remove Ryder or Darrio's cuffs …

"May I speak with you in private, my King?" My chin tips up, perfect posture holds my shoulders back, and I know exactly how proper I look right now.

Every single person looks at me. Even Anna sits aside her inspection of her fascinating red wine to give me the attention I apparently deserve.

His lips part, drawing attention to the thinly trimmed facial hair lining his features. A beat passes before he finally says, "Of course."

I meet Darrio's eyes and I nod to him. It's that easy.

Somewhere along the lines, trust was accidentally formed between Darrio and I.

He turns and leaves the room without question. He has faith in me. I can't ruin that.

Ryder slips his hand in mine and pulls me to the door. My boots scuff the floor as I trail after him.

With a hushed tone, he leans into me. "Humans don't understand how it works. They see your scars even though they aren't darkened. They know you're fae. They have no idea how the powers of a half fae work. Do not tell them. You're powerless until you enter Hopeless waters, but just ..."

"Ryder." I snap his name out, interrupting his long lecture.

"What?" Worry lines his face as he stares down at me.

"I'm not an idiot," I say before shoving hard at the ridges of his back.

I see him shake his head before joining Darrio in the empty hall.

The sound of hushed anger whispers through the room and I wait patiently at the door for the other two women to exit.

The tone grows louder and I turn to see Tristan gripping Anna's wrist and leading her to the door.

"Your insecurities will still be waiting for me after this meeting, I'm sure." He releases her with a hard shove and she staggers out into the hall. Neither fae men move to assist her.

131

Darrio stands with his brows raised high and Ryder simply holds his hands behind his back as if nothing out of the ordinary is happening here. For a moment, Tristan's gaze meets Darrio's and the fae's eyes gleam with unshed power. A ripple of shining color highlights his stormy eyes.

"If you touch my human like that," Darrio cocks his head just slightly, "you won't have a head for that pretty little crown, my King."

I force the smile not to touch my lips but I can't force the arousal from swarming through me.

An odd look passes over the king and I wonder if the word human confuses him. Tristan clears his throat and pulls nervously at the cuffs of the sleeves of his white button-down shirt.

Without replying, he gently closes the door and offers me a generic smile.

"Shall we?" He nods back to the table at the center of the long room.

"I think you are forgetting someone," I say without looking at his mother who hasn't moved an inch.

She plotted this. She's the reason I'm here at all. She imprisoned her own step son for over a year just to get to me.

And, most importantly, she's the reason my father died when I was only sixteen.

I guess in a way, she made me who I am today.

There's no way I'm sitting across from her without slitting her wrinkled throat. A serene smile passes her way as I beam affectionately across the room at her.

A new wrinkle creases her brow as her blue eyes shift from me to her son.

"If you will excuse us, Mother." Tristan waves a careless hand toward the door and my polite smile turns wolfish.

I'm all but bubbling with evil laughter. Manic happiness floods my senses.

Her lips part but only a small breath escapes, her thin hands sweeping down the front of her dark gown.

Push all you like, but those eternal wrinkles won't wipe away, darling.

Quietly, Tristan reopens the door for her and Ryder, Darrio, and Anna all stand just as they were.

The king's mother holds my gaze as she passes. It doesn't deter my shining happiness. She has no idea this is only the first tiny step in a long, vengeful life I'll lead with her. No, no, this is only the start.

"Is your magic at all tangible even with the cuffs on?" Her eyes search mine.

For a moment, I consider telling her of course not, that the great and powerful—slightly nonexistent—magic that courses through my veins is entirely shut away with the cuffs on.

But where would the fun in that be?

My hands shift from behind my back and I pull something from the waist of my jeans.

"I have a faded amount of abilities." I feel the heavy press of attention on me but I don't acknowledge them. Not even Darrio and Ryder. I keep my eyes firmly locked on hers. "I have the ability to take the things that are near and dear to your heart."

With a dramatic wave, I bring my hand above her face and let the thin gold chain swing down from my palm. She's worn it each time I've seen her. She's clung to it like an obsession.

And I've noticed.

Her eyes flare as she sees her own gold pendant

in my hand.

Her pale hands clasp around it with a gasp leaving her lips. Deliberately I lean into her, my eyes boring into hers.

"Be careful, King's Mother. Be very, very careful." I have to physically purse my lips to keep the deranged happiness from spreading across my face from the fearful look she's giving me.

Without another word, I step past her. Carelessly, I begin to walk the length of the room. My fingers trail over the worn spines of books. Dark ash coats my fingertips. The door closes with a pronounced clicking sound and I continue to pretend to be aloof.

And Tristan indulges my performance.

If I'm being honest, I need space from him. I don't trust him and the more space that separates him and I, the better.

Plus, there's that knight's armor at the opposite end of the room. The promising sword is only a few feet away from me if needed.

Once the span of the enormous room separates us, I pull out a large book from a middle shelf. It's completely at random and to my surprise, it's *Alice's Adventures in Wonderland.*

Poor fucking Alice always being thrown into bizarre realms before she's ready.

I flip a few pages and I let my confident voice ring out through the room.

"I want to do this powerful kingdom justice, my King."

He doesn't move closer to me. He simply pulls his hands behind his back.

"I think we want the same things, your Eminence."

Your Eminence. Gods above, if Lady Ivory could see me now. I'm a stumbling juggling act of godly proportions.

"I like you, Tristan." A smile warms my features as I look up at him. "My magic is most powerful on the seventh eve of the full moon."

The moon. It can barely be seen among the smoke and clouds any more. It's barely even noticed in this burning city.

Does he know how to tell precisely how many eves we are from a full moon? Me fucking either.

I'm counting on our high and mighty king to be as clueless as I am.

"Really?" he says in an excited breath. "When exactly is the seventh eve? Have we missed it this month?"

That smile on my lips raises a little higher, a little more genuine. I knew I could count on his ignorance if nothing else.

I'll need a little time to actually put a plan into place. Currently I'm just bullshitting my way through this entire meeting. Through life. I'm bullshitting my way through life, if I'm being honest.

"We are in luck." The book closes with a flurry of gray dust before I slip it back into its proper place. "Two nights from tonight is the seventh eve."

The seventh, the twelfth, the fifty-first for all I fucking know.

His steps stalk closer to me. My eyes never leave his as I mentally calculate how many paces I'd need to reach the knights sword.

Three.

One if I flung myself.

In this moment, I feel a little like the rabbit who taunted the wolf one too many times.

I insisted we be alone. I used this persona to lure him here, to twist his perception of me into something of trust and power.

The narrow span of his thin chest brushes my arm as he lowers his head down to mine.

"I prayed for you," he says on a confessional whisper that fans across my tightly strung neck. There's something dark within the king. I feel it radiating off of him like the ancient and abandoned magic that pollutes this earth. "My mother said if I gave up all that I loved then the world would be returned to me. That I would be rewarded beyond my wildest dreams." Long fingers toy with the ends of my hair.

I wish I knew exactly how I get myself into these situations. How did a lonely thief end up sharing a bed with two mythical fae men every night? How'd that same thief become the obsession of the most powerful mortal man in this country? How the hell did they all let me become the Eminence with zero reference checks?

Brilliant fucking stupidity is all I can blame.

I stupidly fell into this all in the most brilliant of ways.

My hips sway as I slip out of his touch and trail

my fingers along the books, circling back to the door. He watches me as I give him coy glances from beneath my long lashes. Cautiously I hide the fear that's pounds through my heart. He simply stares with a demanding yearning in his bright eyes.

"You haven't gotten me yet, my King," I say in an all too promising whisper just before I walk out of the room.

I walk out knowing I have only one chance to escape this kingdom; on the supposed seventh eve of the full moon.

Chapter Twelve
The Numbness

The four of us lounge in my room. Ryder leans against the wall just near the door, he pins me with a hard stare but no one utters a single word.

Daxdyn continues to lie on my bed like a toddler exhausted from a hard day while Darrio sits in a loveseat that appears too small for his large frame. I slip into bed next to Daxdyn and trail my palm down his forearm. Twisting covers lay in a mess between him and me but it doesn't stop the apparent sadness I feel radiating off of him. His face is tilted into the hook of his arm and he seems to be asleep but I doubt he truly is.

I've noticed when he's left alone for hours he sinks back into himself; into whatever consuming darkness resides within him.

"What happened during your meeting, your Eminence?" Ryder's teasing tone breaks the silence and I pull my gaze away from Daxdyn.

The hard headboard meets the back of my hair

140

as I tip my head up to look at the swirling lines on the ceiling.

"I'm not sure really." I suppose I am but what if nothing comes of it? What if, in two days' time, we're all still prisoners of the Kingdom of Juvar?

"You're not sure?"

Gods above is the exiled prince really good at repeating everything I say.

Let's see just how much he likes his little taunting games.

"Did you know she was your brother's wife?"

My tongue sweeps across my lips as I lower my gaze to him. His eyes shine with a knowing look. He feels the provoking tone of my voice, I can see it in his eyes.

He pushes his hands into his pockets. It's a stance I'm becoming familiar with, but I don't know what it means. Slowly, his teeth rake over his lower lip and I wonder if he'll answer my question at all.

"Yes."

Darrio tips his head to the side to look at his friend. Even Daxdyn shifts uneasily but he doesn't move from his comfortable spot.

"Why did you start a relationship with your brother's wife?" My eyes narrow on him.

It's a disgustingly low thing to do.

If I were Ryder, would I have done it?

I chew on all the pros and cons. His brother took his title. His brother took the crown that was meant for him. His brother lived a life of royalty, while Ryder was thrown into a foreign realm alone and forgotten by his family. His brother—

"He killed my father." Ryder's bright eyes lower until he's studying the chunks of dry dirt on the edges of his dark boots.

Oh.

It takes less than a second for me to decide; I would have done the same thing. I would have taken what was closest to Tristan's heart just to hurt him.

Then I realize how similar Ryder and I really are. Tristan killed Ryder's father and Tristan's mother killed my father. He and I are these pathetically broken beings because one family thought they were more powerful than anyone else.

I think I started this conversation because I wanted to torment Ryder for his condescending attitude but now I can't find it in me to continue with the topic.

I should apologize.

"I'm gonna go," Ryder says, shoving off from his spot against the wall. Before anyone can even say good-bye, he's already left.

The door clicks closed behind him and I just stare at it for several seconds.

Darrio stands and I find myself doing the same thing. I cross the room to him and he peeks over my head to where his brother lies.

Warmth brushes over my palm as he tangles his fingers with mine.

We walk quietly to the door, hand in hand. There's all these important thoughts circling my mind but they get pushed aside for one in particular.

No sex tonight?

"What are you thinking?" he asks as he stares down at me. His thumb brushes back and forth against my knuckles.

It's an odd feeling that's alive between us and it's accompanied by an odd look in his sparkling eyes. I lean into him and he kisses my jaw in a sweet and tender way. A shiver shakes through me from the soft feel of his lips followed by the rough feel of his beard.

It's something so unlike him it makes me think surprising and astounding thoughts.

We've spent every night together. He's held me every night. He laughs and smiles and talks as if ...

"Tell me what you're thinking?" he asks again.

"I think you're in love with me."

He pulls back from me with quiet laughter humming through him.

"Hardly." His finger skims across the tip of my nose, a small, sparking jolt tingles through me. It makes him smile. He does that a lot lately; smiles at me as if he actually enjoys my presence.

"It'll be a lot easier on you if you just admit it now, rather than later." I lean into him in a daunting way, my chest brushing his.

He tilts his head down at me. A serious look fills his face, as if it's the first time he's ever really seen me. The scruff of his beard skims my cheek, sending a shiver all through my body. A breath fans across my neck and in the quietest of confessional whispers, he says, "I'm not in love with you, Zakara Storm."

That smile of his taunts me again.

"Keep telling yourself that." I hold his stare even after I pull back out of his reach.

His teeth sink into his lower lip before he opens the door.

"I have to go talk to Ryder. Good night, my human."

"Night, Rio."

That smile of his lights up his eyes into a sexy look that almost has me dragging him back into my room.

The door closes. I force myself to walk away. Opening the wardrobe in the corner, I don't waste any time. I grab the first nightgown I touch and begin to change as I walk toward the bed. It's a thin, white material that stops at my mid-thigh. The soft blankets tease my bare calves and I slouch down until I'm right in front of Daxdyn.

"It's rude to use someone like this, Dax. If you only want me for my bed you could just say so."

He doesn't answer but he does turn his head until his starry eyes are looking up at me. They're a dimmer color tonight. Not filled with shining humor. His eyes are open but unseeing. Uncaring. Unalive.

"What if, eventually, you want to marry?" Daxdyn studies the soft, white sheets as he asks this question. It's as if he doesn't really care about the reply, but I think he does. I can feel the tension in him, the slow bobbing of his throat as he waits for my answer.

I don't even know where that question came from. Does he think I want to marry Darrio?

"I'm not really the marrying type, Dax," I whisper and my stomach sinks as I realize how true that confession is. His fingers thread through mine, clinging tightly to my hand.

I could be. If I tried to be happy with someone, I probably could be.

I could be happy with Darrio. I could be happy with Daxdyn.

I *am* happy with them.

That thought alone scares the hell out of me.

Sarcasm defaults through me and I say the first snarky thing I can think of.

"Besides, I don't know if you've heard, but I'm like the Eminence and stuff. I don't think someone with that title really needs a man in their life." A smirk pulls at my lips and he almost smiles at me as well. "I'll really have my shit together when I become the Eminence."

Lightly, his fingers trail over the Hopeless lines scaring my forearm. From the inside of my elbow down to my wrist, his touch feathers over my skin, sending a shiver all through my body.

He leans up until his chest is brushing mine, and I'm starting to realize my closeness seems to energize him.

"I don't think someone so holy and all-powerful would be affected by my hands on her body," he whispers against my neck, making my thighs clench together.

I clear my throat and the smile is lost as I part my lips with a shaking sigh.

"I'm not affected by you, Daxdyn." My teeth sink into my lip to force myself from breathing out his name.

"Is that so?" His words feather across the crook of my neck before his mouth follows. His tongue sweeps over my flesh and my eyes flutter closed.

"I feel nothing," I say in a trembling voice.

Slowly, his teeth rake across the side of my neck before he kisses it tenderly. His fingers sink into my hip as he holds me to him and continues kissing up the side of my jaw.

"Nothing at all?"

I try to speak but only a whimper comes out.

Hot flicks of his tongue trail down my collarbone and he pushes aside the top of my nightgown, raking his teeth over the top of my breast. The smooth sheet tangles in my legs as I shift beneath his hard body. His hand pushes against the soft material of my short nightgown. Warmth sears through me as his palm travels up my thigh. Slowly his fingertips sneak beneath my clothes, toying with the smooth skin of my hip.

"Tell me you don't need a man. Tell me you don't need me," he mumbles between kisses across my chest.

A terrible smirk fills my features. My lips part and my words come out in a pained and broken sound. "Whatever you're about to do, Daxdyn, I can already do all by myself."

The logical part of my mind is giving me a standing ovation, while my ovaries are crying and throwing a tantrum over my stupid, stupid pride.

His head hangs until it bangs against my sternum. All of his torturous movements come to a halt.

"You're the most frustrating woman I've ever met," he whispers against me.

I force myself not to touch him. If I touch him, I'll push his shirt off, and I just know it'll end with his sexy lips pressed slowly against mine.

Darrio wants me to help his brother. His brother wants me to help him too. And I want to help him in every way possible. It's a dangerous game the three of us are playing.

And it can only end with my heart in worse condition than it already is.

***

I wake with a startle in the middle of the night. Through my balcony windows, the clouds and smoke drift apart just slightly to reveal a perfectly full moon.

I cock a brow at the unusually bright moon. It mocks me with its fullness. I can only hope the king is as oblivious as I hope he is.

Coldness sweeps over my body and I push my palm across the smooth sheet. Nothing meets my fingertips.

I'm alone.

Darrio nor Dax are crowding the bed right now. Most nights they almost strangle me and for once I have every inch of space all to myself.

I hate it.

My body shifts until I'm sitting at the edge of the bed. My calf skims over Daxdyn's shoulder and I find him leaning against the bed. An empty look fills his tired eyes as he stares out at the night sky.

I sink low, the hard floor greeting me as I sit down at his side.

Tightly, my stomach knots around itself and I can't seem to look away from the hollow look in his gaze.

He's like a shell. He's a shell and his vibrant soul seems to be fleeing from his body.

"What do you feel?"

That half smile is right there in place against the stubble of his five o'clock shadow. It's the slightest of smiles. A smile without happiness. A worn look fills his boyish face.

"Nothing," he whispers.

"Nothing?"

"An emptiness mostly. The feelings I have on a day-to-day basis aren't my own. When no one's around I feel ... nothing." His attention drifts to the hardwood floors and that smile falters as his words die off into painful silence.

That's the saddest thing I've ever heard.

"You just always seemed so happy. I can't imagine you actually feel nothing." My words are edged with playfulness and I bump my shoulder into his. Our bodies are aligned, side by side our shoulders, hip and thighs touch. I physically feel his sadness seeping into me.

"It's easy to feign happiness, Kara. Imagine how boring I'd be if I let my emotions rule my personality. I'd be Darrio, basically." His gaze drifts back to me and it's then that I see it; the force he holds in his joking smile, the way it doesn't touch his beautiful eyes, the sound of sadness clawing at his voice.

It shatters me. His emotions shatter my heart into tiny shards of pain.

"And you always feel this way?"

"Mostly. It's harder with the cuffs on. My own emotions are all I have."

"Right now? You feel this way right now?" Closer, I lean into him.

His empty eyes hold mine as he nods quietly.

My stomach twists and I try to blink back the stinging pity I feel for him.

He doesn't need my shitty emotions clouding up his already depressed energy.

I want nothing more than to change the way he feels. The feelings he's gifted to me in the past flood through my mind. I wish I could do for him what he does for everyone else.

The soft sheet fists in my hand as I hold onto the bed and swivel myself until I'm straddling him. I'm bare beneath my nightgown and I think he knows it. His brows rise with that cheeky smile he always holds.

That false happiness.

The sharp stubble of his beard meets my fingertips as I hold his jaw in my palms. I force him to look up at me.

"Tell me what you feel." I search his shining eyes.

A humming noise rumbles through his chest as he pretends to think about it. The strong feel of his hands on my hips sends a shiver through my body and I push my fingers through his soft hair.

"A steady spike of adrenaline."

"And?"

The simple shake of his head hurts me like he's slicing open my heart to steal what little love I possess.

"Nothing. It's hard to explain, really. It takes a lot to push back the numbness. I find my mind wandering to that feeling a lot lately. It's hard to tear away from it. At night it's … suffocating."

"Tell me what it takes." My lips purse as I stare at him, trying to drown the grief that's clawing up my throat.

His thumbs drift along my hip and several seconds pass without his reply. His attention slowly drifts to my lips and then to my eyes before coming back to my lips again.

The way he's looking at me causes a thousand emotions to drill into me at once and I can't tell if they're my own or his.

He leans up, his head tilting toward mine hesitantly. The heat in his eyes mirrors my own wants and desires. My thighs clench around his hips just as his lips brush mine. The way his mouth skims mine sends a tingling feeling all through my body.

My breath catches and he pulls back too quickly. Soft hair presses to my temple as he leans into me, our warm breaths mingling.

"That. That wakes me up inside," he whispers in a heavy breath.

It's a statement that could destroy me from the inside out. My heart pounds so hard against my chest, it might break.

Daxdyn Riles is a man who causes nothing but heartbreak.

But it doesn't stop me from slamming my mouth back against his.

A low growl falls from his lips as they open and his tongue slips against mine in a frantic feel of pleasure and pain and lust and desire and a mixture of emotions I can't even begin to understand.

Cold fingers skim across my bare hips and up my abdomen. Without warning he pulls at the thin night gown, breaking our kiss just long enough to pull the material off. But it isn't enough. I shove at his wrinkled shirt. Our lips part once more while he pulls the shirt over his head.

When the hard muscle of his chest skims over the peaks of my nipples, I moan into his mouth. At the same time, he shoves down on my hips until my wet center is against the hard bulge of his jeans.

"Fuck, Kara," he says in a shaking breath.

His hips rock against mine as my eyes flutter closed with a building feeling swirling through me.

"Daxdyn," I whisper.

"Fuck, say that again."

His mouth nips at the soft skin at the base of my neck. I feel his fingers skim low across my stomach as he unsnaps his jeans.

"Daxdyn," I repeat quietly and all the racing emotions in me tumble down into guilt that lies heavily at the pit of my stomach.

"Daxdyn," I say one more time and the lust in my voice is entirely gone, replaced with hard realization. He stops, his head tipping toward mine. "I ... " My teeth roll over my lip as pain strikes through my chest. "I'm such a fuck up."

I just asked Darrio if he loved me less than twelve hours ago and now I'm sitting naked in his brother's lap.

Of course, he doesn't love me. I make it

impossible for anyone to love me.

"I'm sorry," I say and my eyes sting as tears threaten to push down my cheeks.

I refuse to cry. Confusion isn't a good enough reason to cry.

"Don't cry, Kara. I'm sorry." His warm hands push up and down my spine.

When I blink, a slow tear trails down my cheek but I still won't admit to myself that I'm crying. He studies it for a moment before pressing a kiss there. It's a sweet feeling that reminds me he was the one that held me when I thought I was dying.

Daxdyn and I might always share that connection.

For the rest of our lives.

My eyes flutter closed and another quiet tear trails down, slowly meeting the angle of my jaw. He kisses there too, drying my tears with his kiss.

The final tear falls, it trails down my face, and he lets it. He waits until it falls, landing atop my breast before he kisses slowly there. The hot feel of his tongue sweeping across the top of my breast has me arching into him. Lower his mouth skims until warm breath is fanning across my nipple and a sharp gasp tears through me as he seals his mouth over the peak and flicks his tongue across my sensitive mound.

My fingers thread through his dark hair and I hold him there as my hips begin to rock against the hard length hidden beneath his jeans.

In a reckless haste, he lifts his hips just long enough to shove his jeans down his thighs.

Then his lips seal against mine in a rush of teeth and tongues. I rise over him and feel his head slick against my sex.

He groans into my mouth.

"Fuck, you feel good." His hand pushes between us as he strokes his fingers up and then down. I gasp against his mouth and he takes that moment to rake his teeth across my lower lip.

"Say what you're thinking," he demands.

A tremor shakes through my body as his thumb circles my clit.

Suddenly my throat feels dry. I've said dirty things, both during and not during sex. But the way he puts me on the spot drives stage fright through me like I've never felt before.

"I—I don't know." Not a single understandable

thought is stumbling through my mind with his hands on my body.

His other hand is like a whisper against my spine as he skims up to thread his fingers through my hair and grips the roots lightly.

Hot breath fans across my lips as he speaks, "I live for emotions, Kara. Tell me what dirty thoughts circle that pretty little head of yours."

Harder he circles my clit and I find myself grinding against his palm while he waits for me to speak all the terrible things that constantly cross my mind.

I'm not shy but the demand in his tone makes it hard for me to think straight.

"I want you to fuck me," I remember how he liked the way I said his name earlier, "Fuck me please, Daxdyn."

His sparking gaze holds mine just as he pulls me to him, his mouth claiming mine at the same time as his hand slips away. I nearly protest, pulling back from him, when the tip of his dick teases my entrance.

I kiss him leisurely, guiding our pace just as I slowly lower myself down his throbbing dick. His groan matches my own as he fills me completely and I settle there for just a second, finding total pleasure in the way he feels deep inside me.

His jaw clenches so tightly it tics beneath my touch. Warm palms grip my hips tightly before they travel low on my ass.

I'm controlling our kiss but Daxdyn wastes no time controlling my body. His hips roll against mine as he guides me up and then down the length of his dick.

"You feel fucking amazing," he whispers on a shaking breath against my lips.

It's slow.

Torturously slow.

We fuck like we'll stay here together forever.

Stroke for stroke he meets me in long even thrusts that has my lips parting without sound against his mouth.

I can't manage anything but gasping breaths.

Coiling energy tightens in my core and it's like he feels every single thing within me.

"Kara." My name is a pained groan that has me moaning in response. Gods above, I love the way he says my name. "Come for me," he begs, his lips skimming over my jaw before his teeth scraping across my neck.

His pace quickens, his hips slamming against mine. Just before it happens, his mouth seals to mine as if he can sense my orgasm, as if my pleasure is his own.

Because it is. Empathically he seems to harbor each intense emotion that swirls within me.

A low growl hums through him just as I clench around his length, making sure I feel every inch of his hardness deep within me. He stiffens in my arms but continues to kiss me. The pulse of his dick sends another thrilling shiver through me.

I've never orgasmed at the same time as anyone before and the intimacy of it takes every ounce of energy in me. I can't do anything but cling to this beautiful man.

Will it always feel like this? Will every time we have sex feel like this amazing, heart pounding ecstasy?

Or is it this simply a one-time thing? Is the forbidden aspect of our relationship what has my emotions filling my chest with intensity?

Maybe I'll never know.

Finally, we part, his head leaning against mine, my hands still gripping his soft hair.

For a few seconds, we only stare at one another, the moonlight streaking across the sharp angles of his jaw, filling his eyes with quicksilver.

"What do you feel now?" I ask breathlessly, searching his gaze.

He licks his lips with a shaking breath. Strength surrounds me as he holds me against his body. A smile tilts his mouth.

"Everything."

Chapter Thirteen
Make a Choice

When I wake, Darrio's staring down on me. I think I can physically feel his gaze on me long before I open my eyes to him. I shift beneath the heavy blankets and sit up to find myself naked and alone in the large bed. The fluff of the comforter meets my chin as I hug the soft blanket to my chest.

Daxdyn leans against the beam of the footboard, the carved detail of the frame spirals up on all four sides and is just tall enough to meet his bare chest. His jeans are slung low on his hips as if he rushed to pull them on.

Darrio stands at the edge, just a foot from me. If I dared, I could reach out and touch his thigh. I don't. I don't dare move an inch.

"I—I like you, Kara. Fuck, why do I like you?" Darrio shakes his head at me and he appears genuinely stunned and confused about his feelings for me.

"I don't know," I say in a quiet voice, my

attention drifting to the white threaded pattern that swirls across my blanket.

Of all the things I thought I'd have to worry about in my life, I never thought it'd be men.

"We think it's best for everyone if you just choose," Darrio finally says.

His words circle my mind and finally I pull my attention up to him. A thin line creases my brows and I'm no longer holding the blanket to my chest as my arms fold over it. My eyes narrow a little on him.

"Between the two of you?" I ask, my features hardening as he nods to me.

Is he serious right now? Right now, while I'm a prisoner of Juvar, I really have to have this conversation? It's as if my magical vagina truly does hold the sorcery King Tristan claimed it did. I must have somehow fucked everything up all on my own.

I let all of one second pass to make it appear as if I'm truly considering their request.

"No."

Daxdyn gapes at me and his attention swings to his brother as if to ask if I'm allowed to do that.

"*No?*" Darrio repeats.

"You two aren't the only ones in this relationship. If you two want to go jerk each other off as a loving couple, that's great, but until then, I get a say in our relationship." My features smooth into a look of virginal innocence. "My emotions are fragile." My hand darts up to my chest to feign emotions in my apparently delicate heart and Darrio cocks a brow at me. "You two are just as responsible for our overcrowded relationship as I am. I didn't manipulate your dicks." I shake my head at them. "You two choose who will stay and who will go."

"That's not how this works." Darrio folds his muscular arms across his chest, mirroring my determination.

The long locks curled sweetly around my face shift as I tilt my chin at him with a look of pure innocence. I refuse. I refuse to let them pin this cluster fuck on me. They're grown men. They can step up and take responsibility like men.

"If our roles were reversed, and there were two of me, would you be able to choose so easily?"

A smirking look fills Darrio's features and he leans in a little closer. He gets right in my face with that brooding confidence that always seems to cling to him.

"If there were two of you, one of you would have killed me the moment we met."

I do my best to bite back the smile that's threatening my lips.

He's not wrong.

"I'm not choosing."

I shove the blankets off with storming anger and stand, my body brushing past Darrio. Just because I can, I give a nice, long—naked—stretch before the two of them.

This is the prize, boys.

Figure out your lives and it could be yours.

Until then, the Eminence has real shit to worry about.

***

Tension surrounds the three of us. For whatever reason, Darrio and Daxdyn don't leave me. The two of them talk quietly while I stand on the balcony overlooking the city. The fires aren't burning here near the kingdom. The kingdom appears contained. Only a blazing red hue lines the horizon as if an unearthly glow is radiating from our terrible planet.

My father worked for the king when I was younger. I grew up here in this city. I could really leave this place. I could leave it all behind forever. If I could only figure out how. Tomorrow night Tristan believes I'll renew this kingdom into greatness.

If I don't have a plan ready by then, he and I will both be in for an undramatic surprise.

Warm hands push across my abdomen and I feel his body against mine. I close my eyes and know who it is without turning to him.

"Come sit with us. Stop worrying so much." Daxdyn presses a soft kiss to the crown of my head.

If I'm being honest, I'm subtly avoiding the two of them in this ridiculously small room.

"He's not mad. Come sit with us. Talk with us," he says again as his mouth presses warmly to the base of my neck.

Daxdyn was never the one I was truly afraid of hurting. He shares his emotions with everyone. Sharing me hasn't ever seemed like an issue for him.

"I'm ruining your relationship with your brother."

Rumbling laughter skims across my neck, making me shiver in his arms.

"Nothing will ever ruin our relationship, Kara. It's just not possible. I've never cared about anyone other than myself and my brother." He pauses, his voice lowering so quietly I barely hear him. "Until I met you."

I turn in his arms and his bright eyes shine into mine.

"Come sit with us," he repeats softly with a smile.

"Kara, come fucking sit with us. You're awful at confrontation." Darrio's booming voice echoes up the high ceilings and I hide my face in Daxdyn's chest as I smile.

I let him pull me back into the room. Darrio's legs are spread wide as he sits in one of the loveseats.

The bed dips as I take a seat at the foot of it.

Daxdyn leans against the beam of the footboard at my side.

"So ... " Darrio's right, I'm terrible with

confrontation, but I'm even worse at keeping my big mouth shut. "Have you two ever shared a woman before?" The two of them both study me with confusion tingeing their identical eyes. "Like at the *same time*," I say with hidden meaning.

At the discreet mention of a threesome, Darrio's spine stiffens more so than usual.

A nagging voice in me tells me to shut the hell up and to not push my luck, but another voice, a voice that sounds suspiciously like Lady Ivory's tells me situations like this only happen once in a lifetime.

"I'm not fucking my brother. Sorry to disappoint," Darrio says with a pointed glare at me. A seriousness fills his hard gaze that makes my teeth sink into my lower lip to bite back my laughter.

Daxdyn tilts his head to look at his twin with a cocksure smirk. "Are you afraid to find out that mine's bigger?"

A long puff of annoyance slips from Darrio's lips as he drags his attention to his twin.

"In all our lives, the image of your cock has never crossed my mind. Until now. Thanks for that."

"It takes a lot to get that beautiful image out of your thoughts, trust me," Dax tells him with a wink.

What neither of them seems to realize is there is in fact a non-biased, third party in the room who knows first-hand whose is bigger.

But I just sit back and watch the show.

"Sharing is more Dax and Ryder's thing anyway," Darrio says with a sneering smile thrown his brother's way.

That has me paying a bit more attention than I ever have in my entire life.

"I'm sorry, what the fuck did you just say?" I ask, standing to walk over to him.

I remember Dax and Ryder sharing a bed and I can't seem to imagine the two of them together with a woman.

A woman who isn't me, I mean.

My thigh bumps against Darrio's and his big hand wraps around it, his thumb skimming my sex just slightly, before he pulls hard. His arms wrap around my hips as I fall into his lap.

He studies me for a minute, my heart thundering to life from the feel of his body all

169

around me.

"This should be weird, shouldn't it?" he asks in a quiet tone.

I shake my head at him. It honestly doesn't feel weird.

My hand pushes up his bicep before my fingers tangle through his long locks.

"I want you." My heart strikes hard against my ribs at the sound of his rumbling admission. "Let's just see what happens."

It seems vague. We'll *just see what happens.* But then Darrio leans into me and I find myself forgetting to breathe for a few seconds. "The three of us are friends. We just need to be open with each other." My gutter mind loves the idea of being open with them. Open. Wide open. "I'm willing to try this with you and Ryder and Daxdyn."

I nod before realizing what he just said.

"*What?*" I pull back from him a little. "Ryder and Daxdyn?"

A frown tips his full lips.

"Yeah."

"I'm not fucking Ryder." For some reason

170

outrage rings through my tone as if it's preposterous for him to assume I'm sleeping with Ryder as well as his brother. "Just ... you know ... your brother."

Gods above, I sound like an idiot right now.

"Why would you think that?" I ask.

Darrio and Daxdyn exchange a knowing look that has me pursing my lips at them.

A smile taunts his lips and before he can reply, the door opens and the prince himself walks in as if he was summoned simply from saying his name too many times.

Ryder glances from me wrapped up in Darrio's arms to Daxdyn.

"You have a type," Ryder tells me, his attention shifting from Darrio to Daxdyn before falling heavily on my lips.

I don't miss the way he's watching my mouth. I rake my teeth slowly across my lower lip, biting back my immediate comments. His eyes flare with color before darting away from me.

It's like it's the first time I'm seeing Ryder. This is why Darrio thought I was sleeping with him. I'm not even sure now how I didn't see it before.

They're just too good looking, that's all. My ridiculous hormones are too hyper aware of how attractive these three fae are.

"You think arrogant fae men are my *type*?" I ask in a breathy voice.

The sound of his throat clearing is the only reply he has for a moment.

"I think it's obvious what your type is."

"Maybe you three have a type," I challenge, standing from my comfortable spot in Darrio's lap to cross my arms with a stance that is pure confidence.

"I think you're right. We clearly have a thing for snarky, big mouthed, mortal women." A smile tilts Ryder's lips.

My mouth falls open as if he slapped me with that insult.

"That's enough, Ryder," Darrio says as he stands. His strong body shadows mine.

Ryder's gaze trails up to meet Darrio's and then he, too, is gaping.

"Holy shit, you're in love with her." Ryder's

astounded smile grows wolfish.

An unattractive cackling laugh falls from my mouth.

"Why does everyone keep saying that?" Darrio all but yells back at him.

"Wait 'til you see her as a fae. You'll be chanting your love for her then. Magnified beauty and for that first hour, her new powers will be uncontrollable. Darrio loves nothing more than a loss of control," Daxdyn taunts with a wink.

Darrio shakes his head at them both and I can't help but smirk at him and his pouting.

"So, about that threesome, though." I bite the inside of my cheek as I eagerly wait for a more vivid explanation of what happened.

"Gods above, not the threesome story, please," Darrio says, tipping his head back like he's really pleading for some mercy on his beautiful soul.

"You want the full story or just the dirty details?" Daxdyn pulls my hand until my body's flush with his. My hands lock around the back of his neck.

"I want both."

Daxdyn hums with laughter, his eyes shining as

he stares down at me. Warm fingers skim along my jaw before he pushes my hair back behind my ear.

"Well, it all started with this human woman … " Ryder says in a reminiscing voice.

"Of course it did," Darrio says under his breath as if he's tired of this conversation already. The mattress dips as he flops down in the center of my bed.

And on and on the four of us banter into the night. Until, one by one, they all fall asleep.

Except for me.

My lips press to Daxdyn's and I push his dark hair back from his face. I roll in the bed until I'm facing Darrio and slowly I brush a kiss across his lips. He hums a sound of exhausted approval.

To my unfortunate luck, there was no threesome.

But there was an understanding between us. Somehow, even Ryder's allowed in our strange relationship. In a way, Ryder's always been a part of this relationship. He's just not like Dax and Darrio. He's different. The same but different.

Quietly, I slip from the bed. I pull my boots on and then I kneel next to Ryder's sleeping form, curled up on the tiny, velvet loveseat.

White light streaks across his strong features.

The features of a prince. The full lips of a prince.

My fingers brush over his soft lips as I stare down at him.

If I could be honest with myself, I'd know that I followed these three into this dangerous kingdom for a reason. I wanted to feel like I wasn't alone in this world for once. I wanted to feel like I belonged somewhere.

Now I do. I belong with these three Hopeless fae.

I'll come back for them. After I finish my task tonight, I'll come back for them.

The moment I rail my father's sword through King Tristan's body, I'll come back for them.

Chapter Fourteen

Power is a Dangerous Thing

The clouds lay especially heavy in the heavens tonight. A thick gray color covers the stars and, thank the gods, the moon. The slick grass causes my boots to slip just slightly as I follow quietly behind Tristan.

"I haven't slept a wink since we last spoke." He walks with the arrogance only royalty seems to have. His spine is so stiff I think it might break in half.

And there, at his waist is the one thing I prayed he'd flaunt in my face tonight.

My father's sword.

"I've rested up rather well. I wanted to ensure my powers would be ready for you," I say as if it's the utter truth, as if I haven't actually lost a lot of sleep due to an over active sex life with two hungry fae men.

He opens the door to the place I told him would

possess the most cosmic power.

Cosmic; yes, yes I did steal that word from Ryder.

The door opens to the tower that conceals the Hopeless realm. The echoing sound of our steps circle the room and I stare hard at the bars that cage in the well to the Hopeless city.

If I kill Tristan here, in this secluded, forbidden tower, no one will find him for days. It could give us just enough time to figure out how to break the iron bars over the well.

Tristan pulls an odd-looking, razor like object from his pocket.

"Give me your wrists."

Hesitantly I lift my wrists to him. My heart begins to kick into over drive the moment his hands wrap around mine.

He angles the black blade against the iron cuff and peculiarly it falls away with a hard clanking sound against the brick.

"The Traveler brought us this little gift. It opens and seals these special cuffs he designed for me."

The Traveler made his jailer cuffs for him to

use against his own fae people?

I can't even process that thought.

The other cuff is removed with ease and then he's staring at me with so much intensity I shift away from him.

"You'll do it now, then? You'll correct this kingdom, your Eminence?"

I nod with too much vigor as my wide eyes search the drastically lit room for a weapon. I just need the upper hand for a moment.

Then it occurs to me, I don't need a weapon when I have commanding power.

"Close your eyes, my child," I say as my head tips up with confidence.

He nods with excitement before his piercing blue eyes close.

It's that fucking easy.

Gods above, why do they all make this so damn easy?

My hand doesn't shake as I reach out to the weapon at his side. I nearly feel the hard hilt of it when an unseen energy swirls through me, pulling at me from the inside out.

I turn. The inky swirling water of the Hopeless well churns faster, nearly sloshing over the edge and onto the brick floor.

My lips part as I stare at it with a mysterious feeling pooling through me. My knees give out and I fall there at the edge of the well. My reflection looks back at me in dark, ominous colors.

As if my hands are not my own, they sink into the waters, letting the liquid ripple through my fingers, allowing it to grip ahold of my hands and pull me closer.

Warmth sears through me and my body begins to shake, but I can't let go. I can't pull away. All I can do is enjoy the tingling fire that's burning through my veins. It courses all through me. I feel it racing through me. The sound of my shirt tearing accompanies the scream that releases from my lips and it's then that I tip my head up to see the moon shining down from the open tower above. Perfectly, as if the gods are spotlighting me.

It strikes across the twirling rapids and seems to cast too much color into the room. It's too bright.

I clench my eyes closed from the stark white light as I fall back from the hypnotic pull the waters seem to have on me. Pain shakes through me in violent waves.

With a gasp, I stand. My shoulders hunching with a heavy weight on them.

The room seems brighter than it was before. Tristan seems thinner, more fragile than he was before. Breakable even.

I'm entirely different than I was just seconds ago.

Black, veering marks strike up the inside of my left arm from my wrist to my forearm. My limbs seem slightly longer, the muscle tone more lithe. Even my hair is whiter now.

And, to my horrendous astonishment, heavy ebony wings span the length of my body. Soft, thick feathers meet my fingertips. They're an onyx color, sprouting from my shoulder blades and brushing the dirty floor.

"M—my Eminence," Tristan stutters, breaking my trance. Wide eyes stare at me in complete and total awe.

"Give me my sword, Tristan." The ringing sound of my voice seems to flow with the turning waters at my feet.

His hands shake as he fumbles with the belt on

his tiny hips.

After a moment passes, he flings the belt and all at my feet.

The hilt scrapes across the bricks and I pick it up with care. It weighs my hands just as familiarly as it always did.

My fingers curl around it with meaning and Tristan turns with sudden worry filling his frame.

"I—I freed you," he says as if it's a reminder.

"Yes, but you also imprisoned me." Power tingles through my limbs, my fingers curling and uncurling into my palm.

Carefully, I pull the weapon from his belt. Colors gleam off of my father's blade like I've never seen before. It's as if my vision has been muted my entire mortal life and I'm seeing for the first time.

Then he has the balls to say something I never thought about. "Your men are still under my possession, my Eminence. My mother is keeping a close eye on them while I'm gone."

My jaw tics as I lift my gaze to meet his. He appears to be once again, the ever-confident king of this land.

"Who do you think will be in possession of your mother once you are no longer here, my King?" My lips snap shut as I stare hard at this little sniveling man.

One step after another I come closer and closer to him but he refuses to back down.

Call it stupidity, call it noble, he isn't shriveling away from me.

"I have the power to harm what is near and dear to your heart, my Eminence." The quiet voice isn't nearly as commanding as it should be as she repeats the words I once threatened her with.

My spine stiffens. I turn toward the sound of her quiet voice.

The king's mother shuffles into the light with someone I hadn't expected to see; Ryder stands in front of her, his eyes held on mine. He towers over her small height, his bulky body too tall for her to really maneuver. The king's mother holds a dagger to his ribs in an amateur like way. She holds it like it's a vegetable she's about to carelessly toss into a soup.

What the hell is she doing and, more importantly, why the hell is Ryder indulging her pretend dominance?

To find me.

He's letting her lead him here to find where I was.

Hmm, perhaps the prince is smarter than I typically give him credit for.

Suddenly there are too many people in the room, too many statistics that could go wrong.

I lower my sword and the tension in the woman's shoulders eases but she doesn't lower her weapon.

A look of surrender is all I give them, slowly I drop to my knees, the sword still held firmly in my hands. My head hangs low and I consider every option I have.

"I told you, she'd never destroy our world, Mother. She is our salvation."

Gods above, is he wrong.

I'd burn this place to the ground if it meant the four of us could find our freedom again.

Specifically, I'd burn this place to the ground just to find a sense of peace for what this woman did to my father.

My fingers sweep across the ground, the fine

particles of debris shifting beneath my touch before my fingers slowly wrap around one of the iron bars covering the well. I fist the cold metal in my hand. My teeth grind together and my muscles constrict as I give the bar a hard pull.

With more strength than I ever knew I was capable of, the bars tear from the solid brick ground. Heavy breaths heave through my lungs and in a flash, my wings span the room. They open like a kite on a spring day. Flashing open and catching the minimal amount of air in the small room. As if I've flown my entire life, I fly up with powerful magic coursing through my wingspan. With me, I bring up the rest of the bars covering the Hopeless realm.

It shakes the ground. Brick tears up from the well. The stones topple into the swirling inky water and disappear to whatever lies beneath it.

I keep my balance as I hover above them like a watching angel staring down on the sinners of the world. The bent and deformed bars fall from my hands, the well eating them up until they swirl into the dark depths of the waters. My black wings beat with aggression, shoving too much wind into the small room. Her hair twirls around her aging face and she's all that I see. Smoky strands of black and gray twirl around the aging lines of her piercing blue eyes.

She's the reason I'm here. She's the reason I am who I am today.

And I don't even remember her name.

It's the last logical thought I have before I swoop down on her like an eagle snatching up its prey.

Ryder leaps to the side just in time as I collide into her frail frame. I physically feel the smallest fracture of her arm as a bone snaps beneath my touch. Her back's shoved against the wall and I hold her there.

"My name is Zakara Storm, daughter of the Royal Swordsman, Tomas Storm." She gasps against me, her sapphire eyes shining with fear. My father's name is probably just one soldier among many in her mind.

Faceless. Forgotten.

Her hand grips the dagger and she sinks it into my shoulder but I don't even feel the sting of the blade, only the hot feel of my blood sliding down my arm.

"What you don't realize is you already took what I held nearest and dearest to my heart." I can't resist the rage that's furling within me. Pain shoots through my jaw as I hold it tightly closed.

My heart thunders to life. I consider all the agony this meek, mortal woman has brought me. The cries of my father will forever echo through my thoughts.

Because of her.

"Stop," Tristan pleads, his voice unheard over the soaring sound of my heartbeat filling my ears.

My heartbeat is too loud.

I bring the blade up between us, driving it up through the center of her rib cage. Hot blood seeps through my tightly held fingers. I watch with rapt attention as the life in her eyes fades away into a dull look of death.

A painful feeling stings my chest and I realize I don't feel any better.

This woman's blood coats my hands and yet, my father is no more alive than he was five years ago.

Minutes pass and I'm still staring into her empty eyes.

"Kara, we have to go." I peek at Ryder out of the corner of my eye. "Tristan ran. Soldiers will be here any minute. Either rain down some wrath or let's get the hell out of here."

My eyes close with a shaking breath.

He abandoned his own mother?

What kind of person turns their back on their family?

Then I realize, I ran to save myself as well when my father was murdered.

History simply repeats itself.

My throat feels dry when I swallow down the emotions building in my chest.

"We have to go."

"We can't leave Darrio and Daxdyn," I say, finally releasing the woman, slipping my blade from her body and letting her hit the floor with a solid thud.

"Darrio's on his way, I heard him follow after Alexia took me from your room."

Alexia.

The woman I killed was named Alexia.

I look up to find Darrio's wide shoulders filling the doorway. He stares at me in awe, taking in the tips of my wings to the angled lines scarring my arm. Then he sees my face. I don't know what he sees there but it has him crossing the room to me.

Strong arms wrap around me and I bury my face in his broad chest. My hand, slick with blood, grips the hem of his shirt.

With a heightened sense of hearing, I hear the distinct sound of feet stomping through wet grass. Several of them. Dozens. How many exactly I can't be sure.

Darrio and Ryder still have cuffs circling their wrists.

My fingers wrap around the iron and I pull hard. I put all of my energy into pulling at the metal encompassing Darrio's wrist.

But it doesn't move.

"It's not normal iron, Kara." His hand trails over the glossy black feathers that reach above my head. "Gods above, is she really the Eminence?" He doesn't look away from me. His question goes unanswered.

I can't focus on anything he's saying.

"Where's Dax?"

"He's still in your room."

My lips part as I try to focus on how close the soldiers are.

"I have to get him." My hold tightens on the bloody hilt of my sword.

"You have to go. They'll never let you go if they get their hands on you now, beautiful," Ryder pulls at my hand but I don't budge.

"I'm not leaving him. Mortals aren't a match for me."

"This new power is surging through you right now. Right now, they're not a match for you, but it'll tire out quickly. You're still a new fae," Ryder warns in a stern voice.

"He's right," Darrio says, his hand trailing down the black mark of the Hopeless on my arm to slip his fingers through mine. "Go with Ryder. I'll get Dax and we'll be right behind you."

Ryder nods. Darrio nods. It's as if it's all settled. And before I even have a say in it, Ryder leaps into the swirling well.

The inky waves pull him under, pulling him home.

Finally.

The pale ends of his blonde hair twirl through

the black waters, and it's the last thing I see before he's gone entirely.

I take a few steps closer, looking into the waters in consideration and wonder. Darrio stands at my side.

A silence settles for only a moment before I look up into his beautiful eyes.

I feel all-powerful; magic and power soars through me. And yet, Darrio's strong body still makes me feel delicate.

His hands wrap around my hips, his knuckles grazing the soft feathers of my wings.

"I'm not leaving you two here," I say with a defiant tilt of my chin.

"Yes, you are." A small taunting smile pulls at his lips, distracting me from my deviant attitude. "You were right, though."

My brows pull together in confusion as I hold his gaze.

"About what?"

His head tips down toward mine, eliminating the terrible space that separates his body from mine.

"I *do* love you."

His soft lips brush mine, taking my surprised gasp with him. A euphoric feeling flutters through my chest.

Darrio loves me.

Of all the men I thought might love me in my life, this asshole fae was not one of them.

Tangled hair meets my fingertips as I thread my fingers through his locks, pulling him closer. My body aligns with his in a perfect and warming way. The sword in my hand hangs tiredly at my side now. My breath catches once more when he suddenly leans back from me, his gaze holding mine as his temple rests against my forehead.

A strange look fills his beautiful eyes.

What is he thinking?

With a hard shove, he pushes me into the dark, inky waves.

The thick water seeps right into me, burning through my veins just as my head goes under. A feeling of overwhelming power wraps around my entire body, suffocating me with the weight of it. It claws at my skin until it's all that I see.

The Hopeless realm has an odd way of

welcoming an Eminence home.

Epilogue

Ryder

Stark black wings cover her soft curves like a blanket keeping her safe. Smooth skin has me shoving my hands into my pockets, forcing myself to not touch her beautiful body.

Long lashes fan over her sharp cheekbones as she lies unconscious at my feet, her limbs curled up around herself.

I fully believe Zakara Storm has the ability to restore the world. Even when she was just a fearless mortal, she might have had the power to destroy it.

When I look at her, she isn't the Eminence. She isn't this powerful being everyone's whispered about since before I can even remember.

This beautiful woman isn't that at all.

She's frustrating, and funny, and cunning and strong.

But gods above, she's got a lot to learn if she ever expects to survive in the dangerous world that is the Hopeless realm.

THE END

The Hopeless Series continues! Book three, Hopeless Realm is now available!

.

Also by A.K. Koonce
The Mortals and Mystics Series
Fate of the Hybrid, Prequel
When Fate Aligns, Book one
When Fate Unravels, Book two
When Fate Prevails, Book three

The Resurrection Series
Resurrection Island, Book one

The Royal Harem Series
The Hundred Year Curse
The Curse of the Sea
The Legend of the Cursed Princess

About A.K. Koonce

A.K. Koonce is a USA Today bestselling author. She's a mom by day and a fantasy and paranormal romance writer by night. She keeps her fantastical stories in her mind on an endless loop while she tries her best to focus on her actual life and not that of the spectacular, but demanding, fictional characters who always fill her thoughts.

Printed in Great Britain
by Amazon

83828441R00120